THE ONLY TRUE BIOGRAPHY OF MAE JEMISON, THE FIRST BLACK WOMAN ASTRONAUT IN SPACE

❖ ❖ ❖

BY SNEEZE, HER CAT

❖ ❖ ❖

(With Hardly Any Help From Dan Greenburg)

The Only True Biography of Mae Jemison, the First Black Woman Astronaut in Space

❖ ❖ ❖

By Sneeze, Her Cat

❖ ❖ ❖

(With Hardly Any Help From Dan Greenburg)

FOREWORD
By Dan Greenburg

Although I've lived with cats for many years, I
recently discovered two amazing things about them:
(1) they can actually speak our language if they want
to, and (2) the Feline Historical Society has been
keeping secret records of all human historical events
for centuries. These historical records have been
translated from the original Cattish by members of
the Feline Historical Society.

Cats who kept records for the Feline Historical
Society at first thought they could write by catching
birds and using the ends of their feathers as quill
pens. But unlike humans, cats don't have opposable
thumbs to grip pens, so they ended up dipping their
claws directly into ink and writing. They learned to
let one of their claws grow longer to write with.
If you ever see a cat with one claw longer than the
others and the claw is black at the tip, chances are
the cat is a member of the Feline Historical Society.

Cattish is not a difficult language for humans to learn. Let me give you an example.

<u>Quotation from the Cattish</u>: Meow mowr rare fffft prowl YAW.

<u>Translation into English</u>: Meow means hello, goodbye or peace. Mowr means I was. Rare means feeling upset. Fffft means mad. Prowl means I'm better. Yaw means feed me NOW. So: "Meow mowr rare fffft prowl yaw" means "Hello, I was feeling upset and mad before, but I'm better—feed me NOW."

FOREWORD
By Sneeze

Hello there, I'm Sneeze, Mae Jemison's cat. I'm also her roommate, her best friend, and her biographer.

I wanted to tell you that before I wrote this bio of Mae, she wrote her own. She called hers Find Where the Wind Goes: Moments from My Life, and it's really great.

You might ask, if her own bio is so great, then why am I writing this one? I'll tell you why. Because the Feline Historical Society wants us cats to write our own bios of the great humans that we live with. And, of course, I was excited to tell you about all the amazing things that Mae has done.

For example, Mae got into college at age , which is two years younger than most people. She became an engineer, and not just any engineer, but a chemical engineer, whatever that is. She became a doctor, and she didn't just treat patients who weren't feeling well, but she actually saved people's lives.

When I was a tiny kitten in Sierra Leone, Africa, my mother told me all about the Feline Historical Society and what members of the Society do. A few weeks after I met Mae, my mother introduced me to Wolfie. Wolfie is a big, bossy cat with long, gray fur and a tail as fluffy as a fox's tail. She's one of the editors at the Feline Historical Society who gives cats like me the job of writing bios about their humans. Wolfie will only hire a cat to write about their human if she thinks their human is going to become famous. If you ask me, I think she's a little too impressed by humans who are famous.

Wolfie had heard a lot about Mae and how smart she is. How she got into college when she was . How she became an engineer, and then a doctor. Wolfie hired me to write Mae's bio years before Mae became an astronaut. And when Mae became the first Black woman in the world to go into deep space, Wolfie was so excited you'd have thought it was Wolfie herself who had gone into deep space.

Oh, I should mention that this bio was not something I wrote by dipping a long claw into a bottle of ink. Since I was writing in the twenty-first century, I was able to use Mae's laptop computer. Sometimes I wish it was still the old days because dipping a claw in ink is easier than typing on a

🐾 x 🐾

laptop.

Mae says she named me Sneeze because when she first saw me, I was sneezing. I guess I'm lucky I wasn't pooping.

When we first met in Sierra Leone, it was the warm season and Mae was eating meals at an outdoor table. I started sitting at the table with her, which she seemed to like, so I made it a habit. I ate all the local foods of Sierra Leone, which were stews and spicy sauces over rice.

I'm a large, white cat with touches of silver and gray, and as I grew up, my eyes turned from blue to green. And stews and spicy sauces over rice now burn my mouth, so I can't eat them anymore. Mae and I have lived together for many years. First in Sierra Leone, then in Chicago, then in New York, then in Los Angeles, and now in Houston, which I'm pretty sure is in Texas.

Cats and humans have been friends for over 10,000 years. Most of the cats who have written biographies of their humans for the Feline Historical Society are members of the rare Catus Longevus breed. Our members can live as long as 90 years.

OK, enough about the Feline Historical Society. Let's start with Mae's early life.

CHAPTER 1

Mae's Early Years, Including the Time She Wrecked the Family Car

"So, tell me, Mae," I said, sitting down at her laptop, "when you were a kitten, you . . . Sorry, I meant when you were a little girl, you lived in Alabama, and you were the youngest of three children, right?"

"Right," said Mae, going through the day's mail without looking up at me.

"And your brother Ricky was three years older than you, and your sister Ada Sue was four years older, right?"

"Right," said Mae, turning to look at me. "But I've told you all that stuff already, Sneeze—more than once, in fact."

"I know," I said. "But I'm finally starting to write your bio for the Feline Historical Society, and I'm already three weeks behind schedule. Wolfie's going to be mad at me. Guess I have to cut my snoozing down to 12 hours a day."

"Just don't forget our agreement," said Mae.

"Don't worry," I said. "I won't send a single page of your bio to Wolfie unless you OK it first. Now let me check a few facts. Did you tell me Ada Sue and Ricky were nice to you when you were a baby or not? I forget."

"Yeah, most of the time they were," she said. "But when our mother wasn't looking, they'd sneak into my crib and blow on my belly and tickle me till I couldn't breathe. I would laugh so hard that my belly hurt."

"You once told me you wrecked your father's car," I said. "But I'm pretty sure I'm wrong about how old you were at the time."

"I was two," Mae said.

"Foofy!," I said. "That means 'No, seriously!' in Cattish. How old were you really when you wrecked your father's car?"

"I told you, Sneeze," said Mae. "I was two. My father and mother took me and a couple of their friends shopping. My father pulled into the store's parking lot, and my mother got out quickly to pick up some groceries. She needed help carrying the bags, so my father got out to help her. He left the engine running, since he was only going to be gone a few minutes, and his friends were going to keep an eye on me.

"Well, I had sat beside him many times when he was driving, and I had studied what he was doing, so I decided that I could drive too. I jumped into the front seat, and—"

"—and you drove the car?" I said. "At the age of two? Foofy! Come on, Mae, give me a break! I'm a smart cat, not a dumb bunny."

"Sneeze, I'm telling you the truth," she said. "I'm not kidding you. Before my father's friends could stop me, I got down on the floor with the pedals, and somehow I managed to push in the clutch and put the car in gear. It lurched forward and dented three cars before it stopped. My father was so amazed I got the car to move, and so thankful that nobody got hurt. I was very proud of myself."

"You were certainly a very . . . brave little girl," I said, making a note about driving her father's car, and still not quite believing that she was only two.

"I was always in motion," she said, "jumping, climbing, falling, and dancing. Growing up, I was just like every other kid. I loved space, stars, and dinosaurs. I always knew I wanted to explore, but I also loved dancing. At night I would go outside with my Uncle Louis and look up at the stars, and he would say that they were really suns. He told me they looked so small because they were so many miles away. I didn't understand that, but I loved it."

"And when you were three," I said, making a note of that, "your family moved to Chicago, which you have always considered your hometown. Do you remember what it was like to leave a place like sleepy Alabama and move to a place as big and noisy as Chicago?"

"Chicago was a little scary at first," she said. "It was even scary to get on the train to go there. I remember standing next to the steam engine. Its huge steel wheels were much taller than I was. The engine was hissing steam, and it actually seemed to be alive—like a tremendous black dragon."

"Yowr," I said, which means 'That's scary.'

"It was even scarier when my mother told me that my father wasn't going to be coming with us," she said. "I had noticed that they seemed to be angry with each other lately. My father didn't come to Chicago for several months. I don't know why. I missed him terribly. At first, we moved into my Aunt Mary's and Uncle Tootsie's basement. I didn't like basements. I was afraid of the dark and basements scared me. Also, the basement was a convenient place for Ricky and Ada Sue to terrorize me."

"What did they do?" I asked.

"Lots of stuff," she said, "but their favorite thing was to race up the basement stairs ahead of me, slam the door shut, and lock me into the basement. Then they would turn off the basement lights and leave me trapped and alone in the dark."

"Yowr!" I said. "That's scary."

"I stood frozen on the basement stairs," Mae continued. "My brain still seemed to be working, but my mouth screamed. And my eyes filled with tears. I tried to figure out whether I could get to the bottom of the stairs and turn on the lights before the monster that lived in the coal bin slithered out between the stairs and grabbed my leg. It felt like my heart had stopped beating."

"We cats love basements," I said. "And we're not afraid of the dark."

"Yeah, that's because cats can see in the dark," she said.

"Not in complete darkness we can't," I said. "But we can definitely see in the dark six times better than humans can. Did you really think there were monsters in the basement?"

"Oh, absolutely," she said. "There was no doubt about that in my mind. I just prayed that monsters didn't know how to climb stairs. Then Ada Sue or Ricky would open the basement door and fall on the floor laughing. My heart would start again, and I would vow to beat them to the top of the stairs next time."

"Was that the basement where you fell off the bed?" I asked.

"Right," she said. "And I hit my head on the concrete floor. I hit the floor so hard I couldn't breathe. I saw stars, and they weren't small suns that Uncle Louis told me about. I screamed and cried and swup-swupped."

"You what?" I said.

"Swup-swupped," she said. "You know that noise little kids make when they try to stop crying? Your lips are quivering, you try to breathe and to keep snot from running down your nose? Swup-swup. You don't know that noise?"

"No, I don't," I said. "Little kittens don't swup-

swup, they myew-myew."

"Oh, right," said Mae. "Sometimes I forget you're a cat."

"Sometimes I forget you're not a cat," I said. "So did your swup-swupping make your mother take you to the vet or what? Oh, sorry, I meant to the doctor."

"No," she said. "But when I stopped swup-swupping, it dawned on me that, hey, I was still alive. That I could hit my head on a concrete floor and not be dead. I felt very proud of myself. Not long after my fourth birthday, my father came back to live with us in Chicago. We were all happy about that, but we were tired of living in Aunt Mary's and Uncle Tootsie's basement, so we moved into an apartment in the Stink House."

"The Stink House! What was that?" I asked.

"An apartment building that had only one toilet on each floor," she said, "which was always backing up onto the floor. Ugh!"

"Too bad you didn't have a litter box," I said.

"Right," she said. "Anyway, we only lived in the Stink House for two months. Then we moved to an apartment where I could go to nursery school."

"I think you told me you didn't like your nursery school teacher," I said. "Am I right about that?"

"No, Sneeze, my nursery school teacher was OK," she said. "It was my kindergarten teacher that I didn't like. She asked me what I wanted to be when I grew up. I said I wanted to be a scientist. 'Don't you mean a nurse, dear?' she answered. Not that there's anything wrong with being a nurse, but what she meant was that she couldn't imagine a little Black girl growing up to be a scientist. So, I just put my hands on my hips and said, 'No, I mean a scientist.'"

"How did you get so interested in science?" I asked.

"My mother played a big part in that," Mae said. "She taught English and math in elementary school, and she knew how I loved science. When I was a little girl, I got a splinter into my thumb and it became infected. My mother turned this into a learning experience. We made a project about pus, the yucky yellowish stuff that builds up when the body fights germs in skin infections.

"But I didn't just want to be a scientist," she said. "I wanted to be a fashion designer. I wanted to be an architect. I wanted to be a dancer. I loved art. I learned how to paint and draw, but ceramics class was particularly fascinating. And then I did a lot of experimenting on how to make the best mud pies."

"What did you love best?" I asked.

"Dancing," she said. "I loved it so much, I thought I might become a professional dancer when I grew up. When I was eight, my mother enrolled me in ballet class. To get to the class, I had to take an elevated train. My mother said I should go there alone. The train tracks were on a platform high over the street. I remember standing on the elevated train platform, waiting for the train, and trying not to look down at the street below."

"Why?" I said.

"Because I was afraid of heights," she said.

I gave her a funny look.

"I know, I know," she said. "An astronaut who's afraid of heights, right?"

"Right," I said.

"I was a scaredy-cat when I was a little girl," she said.

"We cats hate the word scaredy-cat," I said.

"Sorry," she said. "I was a real chicken. I was always amazed when people called me brave. I only tried to do dangerous things because I was curious. It wasn't that I didn't have any fear. I just needed to know about things. But once I got into the astronaut training program, there was no way I wasn't going to get through it because of my fear of heights. It was just something I had to get over, and so I did. My curiosity was stronger than my fear.

"The Apollo 11 mission landed the first two men on the moon and brought them back safely," she continued. "Everybody became thrilled about space, but I remember being irritated that there were no women astronauts. People tried to explain to me why that was, but I didn't buy it."

"Why not?" I said.

"Because in those days," said Mae, "people just didn't think that being an astronaut, like a lot of things that men did, was something that a woman could do. Before they were astronauts, most of these men had been fighter pilots, and in those days there weren't any women fighter pilots or any other kind of pilots. Now there are tons of women pilots, including fighter pilots.

"I always thought that when I grew up I would go into space," she said. "I figured by that time, people would be going into space as easily as they went to work. I thought it would be easy to become an astronaut."

CHAPTER 2

What Are Cats Most Afraid of?

One day Mae asked me, "Sneeze, what are cats most afraid of?"

"I don't know what most cats are afraid of, Mae," I said, "but I'm most afraid of certain animals I met in Africa, like crocodiles, lions, and puff adder snakes."

"Oh, everybody is afraid of those," she said. "I meant the silly things that cats are afraid of, things that aren't at all dangerous. Like vacuum cleaners, balloons, bananas, and cucumbers."

"Cucumbers?" I said. "I'm not afraid of cucumbers. Why would a cat be afraid of a stupid cucumber?"

"Because," she said, "a cucumber looks enough like a snake that seeing one awakens a cat's built-in fear of snakes which has kept them away from poisonous snakes for thousands of years."

"That's crazy," I said. But the more I thought

about it, I had to admit that cucumbers did look
a little like snakes, and that I wouldn't want to get
too close to one. Which makes me want to tell you
what I learned in Sierra Leone about the dangerous
animals of Africa.

To begin, what do you think is the biggest killer
of people in Africa – a lion? A puff adder? A
crocodile? Nope. The biggest killer of people in
Africa is . . . the mosquito. And that gives me an
idea:

<u>Sneeze's Guide to Africa's Most Dangerous
Animals</u>

<u>Mosquitoes</u> who carry malaria parasites kill over
a million Africans every year. That's more than any
animal in Africa. A fifth of all childhood deaths
in Africa are caused by malaria mosquitoes. Mama
mosquitoes feed malaria parasites to their babies, and
it doesn't make them sick at all.

<u>Nile crocodiles</u> are the largest crocs in Africa and
they can be found in almost every river and lake
there. Nile crocodiles are man eaters, but they also
eat women, and they kill about 200 people a year.
But crocs can live without food for months, so if
they can't find anybody to eat for a few weeks, don't
worry about them.

<u>Puff adder</u> venom is powerful enough to kill
a grown man with one bite. They're considered

Africa's deadliest snake. The puff adder probably causes more human deaths than any other snake. It depends on its camouflage to avoid being seen, which means that instead of fleeing from approaching people, it lies on the ground without moving at all. A puff adder attacks only when it's accidentally stepped on. It was named puff adder because before it bites, it hisses loudly and puffs up its body like a balloon.

<u>Lions</u> are very social animals. They live in families called prides that contain one or two males, several

females, and their cubs. Females are able to plan the birth of their cubs so they can help each other to raise them. Lionesses do all the hard work of hunting and they usually hunt together to bring down large animals for food.

Lions have few natural predators, but humans are their biggest threat. Poachers and big game hunters who are only looking for trophies have caused the lion population to lose so many animals that lions are now a vulnerable species. The only lions who ever attack humans are either very old, very sick, or starving and no longer able to hunt stronger animals.

Black rhinos will charge at anything they think is threatening them. They have two big, sharp horns on their nose and they can run 35 miles per hour. The largest black rhino on record weighed over 6,380 pounds. Rhinos are right to be scared of humans. As a result of poachers, they're now on the critically endangered list.

Poachers kill rhinos to cut off their horns to sell them to people who think that eating a rhino's ground-up horns will cure their medical problems. Rhino horns are made of the same stuff as your fingernails. It's called keratin and it's also found in horses' hooves and cats' claws. Eating a ground-up rhino horn would do about as much for you as nibbling my claws or your fingernails.

If all poachers wanted was a rhino's horns or
an elephant's tusks, why couldn't they just catch
the animal, give it an injection to put it to sleep for
an hour so they could saw off its horns or tusks
without either killing it or hurting it, and then let it
go? I mean, why kill these animals?

Hippopotamuses kill 500 people a year in Africa,
and they are the deadliest large land animals in the
world. They're huge, but they can run 20 miles
per hour. They're very aggressive and their teeth
can grow to be 20 inches long. Hippos eat more
than 80 pounds of grass a day, especially at night.
Hippos are vegetarians, so they wouldn't dream of
eating you, but try not to get stuck underneath one,
because they can weigh over 7,500 pounds and can
easily crush any human to death.

A herd of hippos is mostly females with one big,
strong male and several smaller males. The biggest
and strongest male is the only one who gets to make
babies with the females. To coax female hippos
of the herd into making babies with him, he pees
and poops all around him or he poops directly on
himself, and blasts out farts so powerful that all the
females in the herd can smell them. If this makes a
female hippo feel so romantic she can't resist him,
she raises her tushy out of the water and showers
him with her own poop. Yuck! I think we should call

them HIPPO-POTTY-MESSES.

I'll tell you the amazing things I learned about elephants a little later, but first I want to tell you the surprising thing that Mae's mother did to scare away a nasty neighborhood gang.

CHAPTER 3

A Gang of Tough Teenaged Boys Terrifies Mae's Brother

"Mae, tell me about that time a gang of boys terrified your brother," I said.

"OK," she said, "we were living in a tough neighborhood on Chicago's South Side. A neighborhood that had gangs of very tough teenage boys. One warm, lazy spring afternoon, when my older brother, Ricky, was 14, I was sitting on the stoop of our house with Ricky and a few of our friends. Six older teenage boys from one of the gangs walked up to us. One of them was carrying a heavy steel chain. Another one of them carried a steel pipe.

"The biggest boy," said Mae, "the one who seemed to be their leader, said something quietly to Ricky. Ricky stood up, but he looked a little unsteady. In a quiet voice that was scarier than if it had been loud, the leader began to insult Ricky."

"What did he say?" I asked.

"I don't know, Sneeze," she said. "He was speaking too quietly for me to hear.

The boys holding the heavy steel chain and the steel pipe fondled their weapons like they were pet rattlesnakes. Our friends forgot how to breathe. We were frozen in place, waiting to see what would happen next.

"Then," said Mae, "a sudden noise behind me made me jump about a foot in the air.

The front door had been flung open. In the doorway stood our mother. She was glaring at the gang members. She was holding a huge silver pistol."

"Yowr!" I said.

"You could almost hear a dozen mouths dropping open," she said.

"'What is going on out here?' our mother demanded. It was in a voice that made me shiver, a creepy voice that I had never heard before.

"'N-nothing, nothing,' said the gang leader, trying hard not to stutter or shake. 'We were just t-talking.'

"'Get away from this house IMMEDIATELY,' said our mother. 'Do not EVER let me see you hoodlums around here again. Do not EVER speak to my son again—EVER—or you will have to deal with me and his father.'

"The boys backed unsteadily away from our mother and her pistol," said Mae. "They were trying hard not to break into a dead run."

🐾   🐾   🐾

Mae was the one who told me about Dr. Martin Luther King, Jr. I had heard his name before, but, like most cats, I didn't know anything about him. Mae said he was an African American minister who became a famous leader of the Civil Rights Movement. She said he was shot to death on April 4, 1968. Even though I'm a cat and I hadn't known who he was, that made me sad.

"When Dr. Martin Luther King, Jr. was killed," Mae said, "riots broke out in cities all over the country, but mostly in the Black neighborhoods of Chicago. The rioters included many teenagers. They broke windows, stole things from stores, and set buildings on fire. Thirty-six major fires broke out between 4:00 p.m. and 10:00 p.m."

"How did Chicago have enough firefighters to handle so many fires?" I said.

"There weren't enough firefighters to control the flames," she said. "Many Black businesses and homes were destroyed. Mayor Daley closed the streets to traffic, stopped the sale of guns, and ordered anyone under the age of 21 to stay inside their homes."

"But your home didn't get destroyed, did it?" I asked.

🐾 21 🐾

"Well, the riots and destruction came very close to our home," Mae said. "Stores only a few blocks away from us were broken into or burned. I felt scared and unsafe, and I stayed indoors.

"They sent more than 10,000 policemen to Chicago," Mae said. "By April 6, two days after Dr. Martin Luther King, Jr. was killed, President Johnson ordered 5,000 soldiers to come to Chicago. And Mayor Daley ordered more than 6,000 Illinois National Guardsmen to come there."

"What is Illinois?" I asked.

"Oh, sorry," she said, "I didn't realize a cat might not know that. Illinois is the state that the city of Chicago is in. Do you know what National Guardsmen are?"

"Of course," I said.

"All right," she said, "what are they?"

"The national people that guard men," I said.

"No, Sneeze," she said. "National Guardsmen are the soldiers in every state that help the police when there are terrible emergencies."

"Oh," I said. "And did the National Guard guys help?"

"Not really," she said. "Mayor Daley told them: 'Shoot to kill anyone who starts fires, and shoot to cripple anyone who steals things from stores.'"

"You're kidding me," I said.

"I wish I was," she said. "The National Guardsmen came marching right past my family's house. I was terrified. I was afraid they would see me. I ran back and forth between our back screen-door and our front picture-window, sneaking panicked peeks at them. They were wearing camouflaged fatigue uniforms, helmets, and combat boots – war clothes. They were marching in single file, holding their rifles out in front of them, ready to shoot.

"My father was still at work," she said. "Would he be safe when he came home or would they shoot him? It was really creepy. The National Guardsmen didn't seem to be there to protect me or my family. Some of them were Black, but I was just as afraid of the Black ones. I heard that children as young as 13 had already been shot and killed during the riots. I felt they would kill me, too."

"They probably would have killed cats, too," I said.

"I don't think they would have killed cats," she said. "Unless the cats were starting fires or stealing things from stores. I was as furious as I was frightened. And I made myself a promise: I would not be frightened like this ever again. I was just as much a part of the United States as these National Guardsmen were. I would expect as much from this country as they did. I was not only willing to contribute to the United States the way they did, but it was my right and my responsibility to do so.

"Although we couldn't let people destroy things," she said, "we didn't have the right to take people's lives or to frighten them the way I was frightened now. I would remember this promise whether I became a chemist, an engineer, a doctor, a member of the Peace Corps, an astronaut, or anything else."

Chapter 4

Black Is Beautiful

Mae entered high school at the age of 12. Humans tell me that this is two years earlier than usual. In her first year of high school, Mae had classes in algebra, English, Russian, geography, art, and physical education. She was very smart, but, believe it or not, in that first year of high school Mae got terrible grades—like a D in gym class and swimming.

I was surprised to hear that humans get taught in school how to swim and that they get graded on it. All of us cats know how to swim, but tigers are the only cats that like water enough to swim in it. The rest of us, like me for example, hate the water. Mae was strong, she was healthy, she was a good dancer and a very good athlete. So how could she have gotten a D in gym class and swimming?

Mae says she had no idea, but it made her mad at herself. She worked hard to improve in both of these areas. She often tries new ways of doing things to see whether she can find a way of doing them better. Like switching which hand she uses to do things.

"I'm a righty," she says. "But sometimes I do things with my left hand just to see if I can. The change is enough to shake things up a little—to see them from a different point of view."

I myself don't have a favorite front paw for doing things, like writing. I don't even know which paw I use the most. So, if I switched to the other paw, it wouldn't shake anything up. What would definitely shake things up is if I tried to do something like write with one of my back paws. I find that if I want to stand on two legs, it works better if I do that with my back paws than my front ones. I just thought you'd like to know that.

Anyway, Mae tried new ways of doing gym exercises and different ways of doing swimming strokes. She asked gym teachers and swimming teachers to coach her after school. She practiced by herself for hours. A year and a half later, she got the best grades in both gym class and swimming.

By now you probably think that Mae was good at everything she tried, or else that she could work hard at anything she wasn't good at and then become the best at it. Well, not always.

Mae told me that her high school decided to put

on a production of the famous musical play West Side Story. That play had two big acting roles for girls. Mae really wanted to win one of these roles. She got copies of the words and music to all the songs that were sung by the two biggest roles for girls. She practiced them until she got every word right.

Although Mae was a pretty good actor and a really great dancer, she was also — sorry about this, Mae — a terrible singer. So, she didn't get either one of the two big roles for girls in West Side Story. She got a much smaller role than what she wanted. She was very disappointed.

Mae's mother and her Uncle Louis often talked with her about what was going on in the world.

"They said it wasn't enough for Black people to be as well-behaved as white people," Mae told me. "They said Black people had to be better. They told me that whatever I wanted to do in life, as a Black person it wasn't enough to be only as good as white people. I had to be twice as good as a white person if I wanted to get anywhere.

"When Miriam Makeba, the South African singer, came to America," Mae said, "she had very short hair. African women had a tradition of wearing their hair short to show the beautiful shape of their heads.

When my mother saw Miriam Makeba, she decided
she wanted our family to celebrate our own natural
beauty. In America in those days, people didn't
seem to think that short curly hair was attractive.
To help people see the beauty of short curly hair,
the expression 'Black is beautiful' soon became very
popular.

"I got my hair cut very short and in a natural Afro
hairdo," Mae remembers. "And so did my mother
and my sister, Ada Sue. I was tall and thin, and many
people thought I was a boy. That didn't bother me at
all."

Like all the cats I know, I don't understand all the
fuss humans make about the fur on the top of their
heads. We cats have fur on our heads and all over
our bodies. Some of us, like Persian cats, have long
fur. Some of us, like Siamese cats, have short fur.
Some of us, like the Sphinx cats or the Cornish Rex
cats, don't have any fur at all. But none of us try to
make our fur longer or shorter, and none of us try
to change its color like humans do. We just lick it as
much as we can to keep it clean.

If you humans licked your fur as much as we do,
it would solve all your hair problems. And please
don't say, "But Sneeze, our tongues are too short to
lick our hair." Just lick the inside of your forearm,
reach up and smear your saliva all over your head

until it's clean.

CHAPTER 5

Mae's Mother Pushes Her into the Most Valuable Experience of Her Life

Mae was not only very smart, she was great at researching—finding out anything that would help her become a chemical engineer, a doctor, an astronaut, a college professor, and all the things she would become.

"How did you learn to be such a great researcher?" I asked her.

Mae sighed and smiled at the memory.

"When I was 15," she said, "my mother began dropping questions on me without warning. Questions that couldn't be answered without doing some research. Her first questions were about sickle cell anemia. I had no idea what sickle cell anemia even was.

"'If you don't know what it is, then you need to look it up,' my mother said. 'You're always talking about space exploration,' she said. 'Why don't you occasionally think about something besides space exploration?'

"I hated that," Mae said. "Whenever my mother wanted me to try something, she didn't tell me what I should do, she just dropped it on the table like a loaf of bread and left the room. I could either pick up the bread and eat it or I could go hungry. I thought that she did this to make me work harder than my teachers made me work at school.

"So I looked up sickle cell anemia in the dictionary," she said. "I learned it was a blood disease that often attacks Afro-Americans. OK, so what was I supposed to do now? Who could I turn to for help with a blood disease? I knew the study of blood diseases was called hematology. I had once been to Cook County Hospital to visit my aunt. Why not call Cook County Hospital and ask to speak to their hematology lab?

"But I don't have the phone number, I told myself. 'OK,' I thought. 'So look it up.' But what should I say once they answer the phone? How about, 'Hi, my name is Mae Jemison. I'm a junior at Morgan Park High School, and I'm working on a science project about sickle cell anemia. I'd like to speak to someone in the hematology lab.'

"OK, but what would I say if a lab technician actually came to the phone then? Well, first of all, I thought, I would have to slow down my breathing.

Then how about repeating my name and school
and that I was working on a science project about
sickle cell anemia? And how about saying that I
love chemistry and biology and that I'm good at lab
work? Yeah, and how about asking if I could come
there and see how a real lab works?'

"A lab technician did answer the phone," Mae
remembered. "He even said it was OK for me to
come there and look around. But I was nervous.
What would I say to this guy once I was there?

"So I went to the hospital, found the hematology
lab on the eighth floor, and met the technician I
had talked to on the phone," she said. "I was glad
to see he was a middle-aged African American man.
That calmed a little of my nervousness. He asked
me what I knew about sickle cell anemia. Because I
had looked it up in the dictionary, I was able to say I
knew that the illness got its name from the red blood
cells of people who had it. Normal red blood cells
are shaped like round donuts without holes. When
people have sickle cell anemia, some of their cells are
shaped like sickles — crescent-shaped tools called
sickles that are used to cut tall grass. The moon
when you see just a quarter of it is sickle shaped.
Instead of moving through the tiny passageways
of the blood system, these sickle-shaped cells
sometimes clumped up and couldn't deliver oxygen

to every part of the body.

"I told him I knew that the disease could be deadly by the time a child became a teenager," Mae said, "and that very few people with sickle cell anemia survive into their twenties. The lab technician seemed impressed. He told me how they diagnosed the disease in the lab. He showed me the equipment they used.

"'If you like,' he said, 'you could come here again if you wanted to learn more.'

"'You mean on a regular basis?' I said, trying to take him up on what may have been only a polite thing to say. 'Like every week?' I added, pushing my luck.

"'Heck,' he answered, 'you could even come in twice a week if you like.'

"I congratulated myself on being pushy. In the next month, the lab technician taught me how to examine a patient's blood sample for sickle cells. The lab technician was impressed at how quickly I was learning these things. So was I.

"Then one day," Mae continued, "I looked up from a test I was performing and saw an old white doctor wearing a white lab coat, a striped tie, and perfectly pressed pants. He looked like a P.I.P. — a Pretty Important Person. He was staring at me as if he had never seen me before. He probably hadn't.

"'How do you do, Miss,' he said in what sounded to me like a German accent.

'I am ze head of ze hematology department, yes? Who vould you be, und vat vould you be doing here in my laboratory?'

"'My name is Mae Jemison,' I answered in a surprisingly steady voice. 'I'm a junior at Morgan Park High School, and I'm working on a science project about sickle cell anemia.'

"'I see,' said the head of the hematology department. "Und tell me, if you please, vat is your hypothesis?'

"I knew truckloads of big words, Sneeze, but I wasn't too sure about hypothesis. I decided it would be cooler not to ask him what it meant."

"What does hypothesis mean?" I asked her.

"Hypothesis means coming up with a statement about what you expect the results of your experiment will be, so you can test it and find out if your idea is true or not true," she said.

"Oh, I knew that," I said.

"No, you didn't," she said, and stuck out her tongue. "I told him I was working on a project I might enter in a science fair. He said, 'Yes, but you haff not answered my question. Vat is your hypothesis?'

"'I'm afraid I don't have one yet,' I said.

"'Aha!' he said. 'If you are going to vork in my lab, you vill haff to get a hypothesis. But first you vill haff to do some research, yes?'

"He suddenly took everything I was working on out of my hands and gave it to the lab technician. I felt like a puppy who had pooped in the wrong place, but I tried hard not to show my humiliation. He told me to look up several scientific papers and to contact the National Institutes of Health, and then he walked away.

"Over the next few months, I spent all my Saturdays and Sundays at the Illinois Institute of Technology Library, looking up papers on sickle cell anemia. I wrote to the National Institutes of Health, and they sent me original scientific articles. Many times, I had to learn other stuff just to really understand a single sentence in a medical journal article," she said. "But when I figured it out, I was really jazzed!'

"I learned that Dr. Linus Pauling, a Nobel Prize winner in chemistry and one of the twentieth century's greatest chemists, had studied sickle cell anemia and had come up with important discoveries about it. I was surprised and delighted to learn that a famous white scientist had actually studied a Black folks' disease. I came up with a few ideas that might prevent blood cells from taking on a sickle shape,

and I tested them myself in the hematology lab. I
got even more jazzed!

"The head of the hematology lab who had
humiliated me only a few months ago now insisted
on examining my progress on my science fair
project. Of course, there were no computers in
those days, so he made me type out what I had been
doing as though I was writing a scientific paper.

"It was really embarrassing when he—someone
who didn't grow up speaking English—corrected
my spelling," Mae told me. "I actually bet him I
was right, and I lost! I learned about statistics and
about art transfer letters—which are little labels
that you stick onto micrographs, photographs
from microscopes, to point out the important
parts. Whew! This guy was tough and he did not
accept things I did that were only 'pretty good.'
He expected excellence from me, and nothing less.
Period.

"I was surprised that this European doctor
showed so much interest in my work, and that
he allowed me to work in his lab. While I was
occasionally intimidated by his knowledge, I always
spoke up and tried even harder to be prepared the
next time. At age 14 and 15, I was being accepted as
his colleague!

"It had all begun as some annoying questions

from my mother about sickle cell anemia," she said. "It caused me to suck up my nervousness about phoning people at the hematology lab and taking the chance of being hung up on. About asking to go there to watch what they were doing and taking the chance of being refused. About being willing to put in a lot of effort to learn how to do scientific research.

"All of this not only put me in touch with people who were willing to take a chance on me," Mae said, "it taught me how to do research and experiments like a scientist, and it even impressed the professional scientists I worked with to accept me as a colleague!

"My mother had pushed me into what turned out to be one of the most valuable experiences of my entire life!"

"And what happened to your high school science project on sickle cell anemia?' I asked her.

"I entered it in the Chicago Public School Science Fair, and it won me an Excellent award," she said. "As a result, I was invited to a city-wide private school science fair as the public school representative. I won first prize."

"Gracko!" I said. "That means 'Congratulations!' in Cattish. Mae, I noticed that when you talked about the head of the hematology lab and the lab technician, you mentioned that the technician was a Black man, and the head of the hematology lab was a white man. And when you talked about Dr. Linus Pauling, you said you were surprised to learn that a famous white chemist had spent time on Black folks' disease."

"Yeah. So?"

"So I was wondering if you'd rather work with or hang with Black people or white people," I said.

"Good question, Sneeze," Mae said. "I have lots of Black friends and lots of white ones. I went to an integrated high school in Chicago, with both Black and white teachers and Black and white students. I didn't choose an integrated high school to 'find myself.' I already knew who I was. And I've always had both Black friends and white ones.

"Once I was walking through our neighborhood on the South Side of Chicago with my friend Kathy, who's white. In the three years since my family moved there, my block had changed from all white to mostly Black. As Kathy and I walked past an older Black teenaged boy sitting on his porch, he called out to me: 'Why don't you hang with your own kind?'

"I thought it was funny he asked me that. Kathy was my kind. She was a smart, athletic, courageous, and out-of-the-box-thinking young woman like me. Kathy was at least as close to 'my kind' as he was."

CHAPTER 6

And Now, Back to African Animals

<u>OK, let's talk elephants and how smart they are:</u> No, wait. Before we talk about elephants, I just learned something about ants that I think will amaze you. Ants? Yes, ants. And you can use this to impress your friends: You probably knew that ants are incredibly strong, right? Well, guess how many times its weight an ant can lift. If you guessed an ant can lift something that's 10 times its own weight, it's more than that. Can an ant lift 50 times its own weight? Well, it's more than that too. Can an ant lift 500 times its own weight? Well, it's even more than that. The answer: An ant can lift 5,000 times its own weight! I bet you can stump your friends with that one.

<u>OK, now let's really talk elephants:</u> First, I'm sure you'd like to know how big elephants are, compared to a car or a house. Well, the average car weighs 4,000 pounds, and the average one-story house is

8 feet tall. The biggest African elephant on record weighed 24,000 pounds—6 times heavier than the average car—and it was 13 feet tall, almost twice as tall as a one-story house. If elephants are bigger than cars or houses, aren't they dangerous? Not really. However, if wild elephants feel threatened or frightened, they've been known to trample people, but that hardly ever happens.

<u>How smart are elephants?</u> Elephants are some of the smartest animals on Earth. Chimpanzees are almost as smart as humans. An article I read in in ABC Science says elephants are as smart as chimpanzees and dolphins. In the past few years, scientists have found that elephants are good at solving problems and at making their own tools. For example, they make small tree branches into switches to shoo away flies, and they use sticks to poke ticks off their skin.

Wild elephants also remember the locations of water holes that are hundreds of miles apart, and they return to them every year. Elephants learn through watching and imitating. In a place like a zoo, they easily learn how to open simple locks. I heard that an elephant in a Korean zoo surprised its keepers by learning to imitate the commands they gave it by sounding out Korean words. Working elephants in Asia wear bells around their necks so their owners can hear where they are at night. Many young elephants stuff their bells with mud so their owners can't hear them, and then they sneak into neighboring fields to eat bananas.

An elephant named Shanthi at the zoo in Washington, D.C. can play the harmonica.

<u>How smart are pigs?</u> Why am I even mentioning pigs in this list of wild African animals? Because I really like pigs and I just learned that scientists who study pigs found that pigs can solve problems as well as chimpanzees do. And they say that pigs are smarter than dogs or 3-year-old children!

Pigs can be trained like dogs and can be taught to come when you call their name. They have long memories and feelings like love and sadness. When pigs are sad, they cry real tears. They are affectionate by nature, and they express happiness and excitement in playfulness. They greet each other by rubbing noses. They talk to each other with over 20 distinct oinks, grunts, snorts, snarls, and squeaks. They love to sleep together, cuddled up nose-to-nose.

Pigs get upset when they see another animal or human suffering. There are many stories of pigs who ignored danger to save a human or animal from drowning or from a fire. One pig stopped a passing car to get help for her human who was having a heart attack.

But aren't pigs just plain dirty? No. Unless you keep them in mud, pigs are very clean animals, so clean they could live in your house like dogs or cats, and they won't poop near where they eat or sleep. So if you wouldn't think of eating your dog, maybe you shouldn't eat ham or bacon either!

OK, enough about pigs. Let's get back to elephants.

Do elephants have feelings like people? Yes.
Elephants are very social animals. They live in herds
of more than 100 animals that are led by females.
Elephant mothers take care of each other's calves
(that's what we call elephant children), and they
form protective circles around their calves whenever
they're threatened by lions or poachers. Female
calves usually stay with the herd for life, while young
males leave it to form their own herds.

Elephant family members talk to each other in
gentle chirps, nudges, kicks, tilting of heads, flapping
of ears, and in rumbling voices that are so low that
people can't hear them and that can travel for miles.
They discuss problems, they make group decisions,
and they celebrate their achievements by trumpeting,
intertwining trunks, and slamming each other's tusks
together.

Wild elephants form strong social bonds. When
they're upset, they comfort each other, and when
one of them dies, they mourn their dead. Wild
elephants even have death rituals. Anthony Hall-
Martin, a South African biologist who studied
elephants for over 8 years, watched the entire family
of a dead female, including her young calf, gently
touching her body with their trunks, trying to lift her.
They were all rumbling loudly. Her young calf was
crying and made sounds that sounded like a scream,

but then the entire herd fell silent. They then began to throw leaves and dirt over the dead elephant's body and broke off tree branches to cover her. They spent the next 2 days quietly standing over her body. They sometimes left to get water or food, but they would always come back to the dead elephant.

I, Sneeze, am proud to be a cat, but I was so impressed by the things I learned about elephants, I wondered if it was too late for me to become one. I asked Mae because she knows everything.

"Sneeze," she said, "I've never heard of a cat who was able to become an elephant. I mean you would have to grow a trunk. And you'd have to put on several thousand pounds."

OK, I decided that would be way too much trouble.

<u>How long do elephants live?</u> In the wild, African elephants can live to be 70 years old, but African elephants born in zoos live an average of only 17 years. The biggest danger to elephants in the wild is from humans and poaching. Twenty years ago, there were a few million wild elephants in Africa. Now there are only about a half million.

Every year, more and more poachers go to Africa to kill elephants for the ivory in their tusks. The US made it a crime to sell ivory, but it's still not a crime to kill elephants for their tusks. Poachers in Africa kill 35,000 wild elephants every year!

I, Sneeze, think that poachers who shoot and kill rhinos and elephants would deserve it if we gave the animals guns so they could shoot back. Or maybe we could get together a few rhinos or elephants to sit on poachers for a few hours and see how they like not being able to breathe. Or, even better, let's get a few 7,500-pound hippopottymesses to drown those poachers in showers of stinky poop.

Chapter 7

Mae Graduates High School and Enters College at a Surprisingly Young Age

In case you think I know all about Mae in college because I was there with her as her cat companion, you're wrong. When Mae went to college, I hadn't even been born yet, and when I was born, it was in Africa. How I know all this is because Mae told me when she met me years later when I was a tiny kitten in Sierra Leone.

When Mae graduated high school in Chicago, she was only 15 years old. Fifteen is pretty old for a cat, but not at all old for a human. Most humans graduate high school when they're 18. Four universities offered Mae scholarships, which meant she didn't have to pay a lot of money to go there. She chose Stanford University in northern California, which she had always wanted to go to. Mostly because they had a great football team. Mae was a huge football fan.

"You know, Mae," I said, "it's too bad that

humans have to go away to college, usually far away from where they live, and spend a lot of money learning what they need to know in life. Cats are born knowing most of what we need to know, and we learn the rest from our mothers. Like how to wash our faces by licking our paws, how to kill things we need to eat, and how to cover our poop. I have never met a newborn human baby that knew how to flush a toilet, to change its own diaper, to give itself a bath, or to kill something it could eat for dinner."

"Um, OK, thanks, Sneeze," she said. "I was about to say that neither I nor any of my family had ever been to California. And as the day for flying to California approached, I began to worry about my parents. Both my older brother, Ricky, and my sister, Ada Sue, had already gone away to college. What would my mom and dad do when their youngest child left home? I hoped they wouldn't worry about me. Telephoning them would be too expensive, but I would write them often. Would I be OK, alone in a faraway place where I didn't know anybody?" she said.

"Of course you would," I said. "You were healthy and smart and you had grown up in a big city, so you were going to be fine."

"Right," she said. "So my parents drove me to Chicago's O'Hare International Airport with my luggage. When I got on the plane for San Francisco, my mother looked sad. My father looked like he was trying hard not to look sad. I was determined I wouldn't cry. Why would I cry? I hadn't cried in at least four years.

"OK, so I was leaving home, but I was excited to be going away to college like Ricky and Ada Sue, wasn't I? I was going to Stanford, the school I had always wanted to go to, wasn't I? I was going to the perfect place to begin a career in engineering and science, a place that would both help me and challenge me.

"When my plane landed at the San Francisco International Airport in California, I went to the baggage claim to pick up my bags. There I was told where to wait for the Stanford bus. A young Black man came up and introduced himself. He was a member of the Stanford Black Student Union and he was helping to welcome the African American students and take them to the campus.

"I got into a van with him and several other students. On the way to the Stanford campus I got an introduction to California freeways. The freeway that the van took from the airport went through the second most traffic-congested region in the country. The Stanford campus was breathtakingly beautiful, with impossibly tall palm trees and gigantic flower beds everywhere I looked. The air was fresh and warm, the buildings, like many buildings in America's Southwest, were tan with roofs of red tiles. Suddenly I heard someone call my name.

"'Mae! Mae!' called the voice. 'Up here!'

"This was weird, because nobody at Stanford even knew me. I looked up and saw a young blonde woman leaning out of a dormitory window and waving. 'I'm Janet, your new roommate!' called the young blonde woman.

"Janet came down and helped me haul my bags upstairs. Janet would turn out to be the best roommate I could have hoped for. She had a great smile and a sunny personality. She was 19, three years older than me, and she was nearly six feet tall. So she was like a big sister—Ada Sue's age, but taller.

"Stanford was the first school to have dormitories with boys and girls on the same floor. I was just 16, the youngest student in the dorm. I was so young that, when I got a traffic ticket while driving a borrowed car, I had to get a grownup, somebody over 18 like Janet, to go with me to juvenile court because my mother and father were far away in Chicago."

Chapter 8

Things People Say About Cats that Annoy Cats Like Me

OK, before we continue my biography about Mae, I just wanted to get something off my chest. The nasty expressions that humans have about cats really get my back up, and I mean my back actually goes up like when a strange cat hisses at me. For example:

<u>Scaredy-cat.</u> Why would you call somebody a scaredy-cat? Why not a scaredy-dog, or a scaredy-man, or a scaredy-squeek-squeek? Squeek-squeek means 'mouse' in Cattish. Every mouse I've ever met has been a scaredy-mouse—scared of me! But I've only known one scaredy-cat, a Siamese named Sheldon. So go ahead and call someone a scaredy-sheldon, if you like.

<u>Not enough room to swing a cat.</u> Why would you ever swing a cat? Are you playing baseball indoors in a tiny room and you don't have any baseball bats? For starters, you shouldn't be playing baseball indoors. You could break windows and lightbulbs

and vases and stuff. Your family will get mad and start yelling. But the most important thing to remember is this: NEVER SWING A CAT!

Now let me tell you a few nice things that are said about cats—by people or cats:

<u>A cat will be your friend, but never your slave.</u> Right. And why do humans give us names and expect us to come when they call us, but when we call them, they pretend they didn't hear us?

Dogs have masters, cats have servants. True. And yet, we cats still haven't been given the right to vote.

Cats are kindly masters, as long as you remember your place. Of course. Seriously, though, what part of "masters" don't you understand?

In ancient Egypt, cats were worshipped as gods. Cats haven't forgotten that. Yeah, and if they had worshipped humans in ancient Egypt, don't think humans would have forgotten that either.

People who hate cats will come back as mice in their next life. A mouse named Melvin actually told me that was true.

OK, we'd better get back to Mae's biography.

CHAPTER 9

Skinny Mae Is a Terror on the Football Field

"Mae," I said, "what made you choose Stanford over the other three colleges who offered you scholarships?"

"As I said before," she answered, "I was a football fanatic. The reason I chose Stanford was that their football team had won the Rose Bowl two years in a row before I got there.

Stanford played razzle-dazzle ball. They used fake punts, fake field goals, and lateral-lateral passes to confuse their opponents."

"As a cat," I said, "I don't understand any of those words and, frankly, I don't care. But somebody told me you actually played football at Stanford. I thought only boys played football in college."

"I did play football at Stanford," she said. "But it wasn't on the varsity team. I played touch football on a dorm team in their intramural dorm league. 'Intramural' means limited to the members of a particular school or college, and 'dorms' are the buildings where we live at school."

We cats don't know what varsity football is, so I had no idea what touch football is, but I'll tell you what Mae told me. Maybe it will make sense to you.

It seems that touch football is played without helmets or shoulder padding. And instead of tackling a player who has the ball, in touch football all you have to do to stop them is to touch them with both hands. To be honest, cats think football is stupid. Instead, we bat around a tinfoil ball or we pounce on things that we pretend are squeek-squeeks in order to practice our hunting skills. That's a lot more serious than what humans do, which I hear is to try to get a ball from one end of a field to the other, and if you don't agree with me, it's because you're probably not a cat.

Both boys and girls were on the Stanford touch football teams. Mae told me that she and a girl named Tammy were the only girls on her dorm team, and the rest were boys.

Mae's first touch football game of the year was against a fraternity team with big, muscular, mean players. Fraternities are clubs some students join that have rooms to live in. Although Mae was skinny and the youngest student in the dorm, she was a very good athlete. So she was used to roughhousing with her brother, and she was surprisingly strong. The first time the largest guy on the fraternity team caught the ball, he tried to scare Mae by rushing right at her.

Instead of scooting out of his way, Mae stood her ground and made a good, solid, hard block. The amazed fraternity guy felt he had run smack into a brick wall.

Mae told me that in college she majored in chemical engineering and African American studies. She also became the head of the Black Students Union.

"What is chemical engineering?" I asked her.

"Well," Mae said, "chemical engineers solve problems that involve the use of chemicals, drugs, food, and other products."

"Oh, right," I said, having no idea what she had said. "Wasn't chemical engineering an unusual thing for a girl to study?"

"Yes," she said. "And I didn't realize how unusual it was that I had begun college two years earlier than most people, or that my parents had let me live so far away from them. Or how hard it would be for a Black woman to study engineering."

"What made that hard?" I asked.

"Because in my classes, some professors would

just pretend I wasn't even there," she said. "I would ask a question and the professor would act as if it was the dumbest question he had ever heard. But when a white guy would ask the same question, the professor would say, 'That's a very clever observation, young man.' People didn't think a Black woman was smart enough to even have an intelligent discussion."

"Cats come in lots of colors, including Black," I said, "but that's never a reason for us not to get along."

"Well, Sneeze," she said, "that's one way that cats are smarter than humans."

"Thanks," I said.

"During my senior year in college," Mae said, "I was trying to decide whether I wanted to go to a medical school or to become a professional dancer. My mother gave me good advice. She said, 'Mae, you can always dance if you're a doctor, but you can't doctor if you're a dancer.'

"I decided to go to medical college," she said, "but I also signed up for dance classes. And I made a little dance studio in my apartment."

CHAPTER 10

Mae Starts Medical School and Is Grossed Out

"After I graduated college at Stanford," Mae told me, "I was accepted at Cornell University Medical College in New York, one of the best medical schools in the country. My first class there was anatomy."

"What's that?" I said.

"It's the study of how people are put together. In anatomy we learned about internal organs and how they work—muscles, blood vessels, nerves, and bones. The way we learned was to cut open the body of a dead person and study it. This kind of carefully cutting apart a body to study it is called dissection."

"Mae, I can't believe you actually cut open a dead person," I said. "And where did you get these bodies? Did you rob graves during a full moon or what?"

"Not quite," Mae said. "In the lecture hall, we were told all about the bodies we were going to study—where they came from, how they were kept from rotting, and so on. Where they came from is that living people left their bodies to the medical college before they died. Why? Because they wanted to help doctors understand diseases and other medical problems by letting medical students study their bodies after they died. We were told that the bodies were kept from rotting with a liquid that preserves dead bodies. Then we were told to change into our white lab coats and go to the anatomy lab to start work on the bodies that were assigned to us."

"Didn't that gross you out?" I asked.

"It sure did," Mae said. 'I thought, Wait, don't you want to at least give us a chance to get used to dead people? Don't you want to explain a little more about dissection? I have never cut into a dead human body. Is the anatomy lab filled with dead human bodies? What if I cut into a dead human body and it screams? What if it reaches out and grabs me with its dead human fingers? Don't you want to tell me what I'm supposed to do then?"

"Yowr!" I said. "This sounds worse than when Ricky and Ada Sue locked you into the basement with its imaginary monsters."

"Oh, it was a lot worse than that basement!" Mae said. "As I walked slowly into the lab, the other students—the real pre-med students—rushed in excitedly. The real pre-med students all wanted to make the first incision—which means the first cut—into the dead body."

"Why do you call them real pre-med students?" I asked.

"Because," she said, "unlike the other pre-med students who wanted to become full-time doctors, I only wanted to be a part-time doctor so I could help people in addition to becoming an engineer, a dancer, and an astronaut. I watched the real pre-med students make careful incisions in the body so they could look around inside it at the organs. After a while I got used to dead bodies and, amazingly, I was even able to make my own incisions."

"Yuck!" I said.

"On our first day in microbiology lab," she said, "we were told we were going to study how our own bodies react to vaccinations."

"What's microbiology?" I asked.

"Oh, sorry," she said. "Microbiology means we studied parts of the body that are so tiny we needed a microscope to see them. We studied how our bodies react when they get vaccinations—which means injections to protect us from getting a disease like typhoid. They said that for this study we would need blood."

"And where were you going to get blood?" I

asked. "Were you going to leap on unsuspecting people and bite them on the necks?"

"No, Sneeze," she said, "we got them from each other. They told us to choose the student sitting closest to us as a lab partner, and to practice drawing blood from each other with a hypodermic needle."

"Are you cool with hypodermic needles?" I asked.

"Are you serious?" she said. "I not only hate hypodermic needles, but my new lab partner looked like he wouldn't even be able to tie his shoes on his first try. You notice things like that when you're about to be stabbed with a two-inch-long hypodermic needle."

"So was he able to draw blood from your arm or what?" I asked.

"Not for the first dozen or so tries," she said. "It's easier to draw blood from someone's arm if their veins are thick enough for the needle sticker to see where to stick the needle. Unfortunately for me, my veins are thin and hard to see. Even experienced doctors and nurses have trouble getting their needles into me on the first try. Even if my lab mate was actually able to tie his shoes, his attempts to give me injections made me feel like a human pin cushion."

"But finally everyone got enough blood from their lab mate's arm to stop the stabbing?" I asked.

"We didn't just stick each other to draw blood for

the experiments," she said. "We also gave each other vaccinations to prevent a disease called typhoid. These vaccinations made you feel hot, headachy, feverish, tired, and like you wanted to puke for about twenty-four hours. They also made your arm that got vaccinated sore for two or three days."

"I'm so glad cats don't go to medical school," I said.

"I got pretty good at giving my classmates injections, vaccinations, and physical examinations," she said. "And I learned how to do all the things that doctors do—listen to someone's heart through a stethoscope, examine their eyes, use a little hammer on their knees to test their reflexes, and so on. I would soon learn that when I became a doctor it was very different to ask complete strangers to take off their clothes so I could examine them naked."

"I don't think I'd have a problem with that," I said. "But I'm a cat, so they probably wouldn't take off their clothes to let me examine them anyway."

"On a summer vacation from medical school," she said, "I volunteered to do some doctoring at a Cambodian refugee camp in Thailand. I was surprised how much I liked helping sick people. So on another summer vacation, I went to Kenya, a country in East Africa. To cover my expenses, I took out a student loan and I got another loan from the

International Travelers Association while I was in Kenya."

"I bet you saw some great wild animals in Kenya," I said.

"I did go to a few game parks," she said. "I saw wild elephants, zebras and lions, but I also had several jobs there. I joined the African Medical Education and Research Foundation, who used to be known as the Flying Doctors. They were a group of doctors who traveled into remote areas of Kenya and East Africa to treat patients with minor ailments and even perform surgery on people who would otherwise have to go without it. They also began to study how the illnesses people had were being spread."

"Why were they called the Flying Doctors?" I asked.

"The Flying Doctors traveled on small planes because the roads were either terrible or they didn't even exist," she said. "When there were no places to land a small plane, we doctors simply walked from house to house in small villages, doing physical exams and giving vaccinations like those I did in med school, but with better aim. Sometimes, like in a clinic near Mt. Kenya, I also helped out in surgery."

"What part of the words 'summer vacation' don't you understand?" I said.

"Come on, Sneeze," she said. "I told you I went to a few game parks and saw elephants, zebras, and lions. I even stopped in the nearby city of Nairobi to have my hair done. When the hairdresser was finished cornrowing my hair, the owner of the shop asked her how much I owed her. The hairdresser did her figuring out loud in Swahili, which was the local language. I speak Russian, Japanese, and Swahili.

"I heard the hairdresser tell the owner in Swahili that she would have to raise the price a little because I had a 'kichwa kubwa,' and 'nyele nyingi'—which means a big head and a lot of hair. When I laughed, everybody in the shop roared with laughter too. Everybody but the hairdresser, that is."

"When I returned to Cornell Medical College," Mae said, "my advisers asked where I wanted to do my doctoring when I finished my internship and residency. I said I wanted to work helping people in developing countries like Africa, and then I wanted to go to graduate school in engineering."

"I bet that went over like a concrete balloon," I said.

"Yeah," she said. "My advisers were shocked. They said I was making a terrible mistake to spend unnecessary time helping people in developing countries and then doing graduate school work in engineering. They begged me not to do that—after all, I was graduating from Cornell, one of the finest medical schools in the country."

"Don't tell me that changed your mind," I said.

"Well, she said, "I was scared by my advisers' reactions, so I did spend the next year as an intern at Los Angeles County Hospital. There I learned how to work 36 hours without sleeping, which would soon turn out to be a valuable skill.

"And when I finally got my MD degree from Cornell Medical College, I applied to several organizations in developing countries as either an engineer or a doctor—whichever they needed most.

"I was accepted as a doctor by the Peace Corps in West Africa. I was the Area Peace Corps Medical Officer for Sierra Leone and Liberia. I was responsible for the health of all the US Peace Corps volunteers, staff members, and embassy personnel of Sierra Leone and the Peace Corps volunteers in Liberia. I managed a laboratory, a medical office, a pharmacy, and volunteer health training. I also acted as the primary care doctor. I was only 26.

"I found myself trying to treat diseases I had only read about in tropical medicine textbooks."

CHAPTER 11

Sneeze's Handy Things to Say in Krio

Krio is the language they speak in Sierra Leone, the country in Western Africa where I was born. Although English is the official language there, more people – over six million of them –– speak Krio than English, and most cats speak Cattish.

If you ever go to Sierra Leone, here are some things you can say in Krio that might come in handy.

Do you speak English?
U sabi tok Inglish?

Is there someone here who speaks English?
Posin de ya we sabi tok Inglish?

I need your help!
Ep me!

It's an emergency!
Na emagency!

Where is the toilet?
Oosye toilet dey?

I don't understand.
Ar nor sabi.

I'm sick.
Ah no well.

Don't touch me!
Leggo me!

Leave me alone!
Yo no go lef me!

Thief!
Teefman!

Stop thief!
A go call police!

Goodnight.
Ar de go sleep.

CHAPTER 12

Mae Becomes a Peace Corps Doctor

For two and a half years, Mae worked as a doctor for Peace Corps volunteers in Sierra Leone, West Africa, with very little equipment or medical supplies or none at all.

What was the weather like in Sierra Leone? When I lived there with my cat mom, and then with Mae, there were only two seasons—a hot one with dry, dusty winds, and a hot one with torrents of rain and flooding.

Most of the Peace Corps volunteers shared houses with a few other volunteers. We shared ours with two Peace Corps medical staff members. It was better than we expected. It had two bedrooms, a dining room, two bathrooms, and a kitchen. It had electric lights instead of kerosene lanterns, and running water instead of a pump, although we did have to boil out the germs and bugs before we drank it.

We also had our own personal live-in watchman. I think everybody had a live-in watchman, because most of these houses had things stolen while people were asleep. The Krio word for thief is "teefman." A teefman would stick a long pole through an open bedroom window that they'd hook onto wallets, purses, or pants with valuable things in the pockets. These stealing poles, as I called them, would have sharp razor blades glued near the end, so if you grabbed the pole you'd cut your hands or your paws.

During the first two weeks that I knew her in Sierra Leone, one of the Peace Corps volunteers, a man, got very sick. Another doctor there said what the man had was malaria, but after the man had been taking a medicine for 24 hours, Mae told me it didn't look like what he had was malaria.

"Malaria is a disease that's common in tropical countries," she told me. "It's spread by mosquito bites. An attack usually starts with shivering and muscle pain, followed by a high fever. This man got worse and worse. I was sure that what he had wasn't malaria, it was meningitis, a swelling of the brain caused by an infection. The symptoms can be similar to malaria. At 2:00 a.m., after a power failure in the hospital, I started rummaging around with a flashlight to try and find him some antibiotics that might treat meningitis.

"If not treated correctly," she said, "meningitis will kill you, and I knew it couldn't be treated correctly in Sierra Leone. So I asked the staff of the US embassy in Sierra Leone to get my patient a military medical flight on an Air Force hospital plane. Then I could take him to a US Air Force hospital in Germany where they could treat him better. The people at the embassy told me that just to start that process going would cost $80,000."

"Yeah, I remember that," I said. "I love what you did next."

"I told them to get the plane ready anyway," she said. "The embassy staff just stared at me. I was only 26, and I looked even younger than that. And yet, here I was, telling them to spend $80,000 to fly this patient to Germany.

"They started questioning whether I had the authority to give them such an order. Surprisingly, after being awake for 36 hours—which I was used to after being an intern in Los Angeles County Hospital—I was very calm and I knew what the issues were. Calmly but firmly, I said, 'Look, I am this man's physician. He is my patient. I do not need anyone's permission to give you that order.'

"They glared at me, probably thinking of me as a pushy young Black girl. But then they ordered the plane, and we put my patient on it. By the time we flew him to Germany and got him admitted to the US Air Force hospital there, I had been staying up with that patient for 56 hours without sleep. Of course, he survived."

CHAPTER 13

Mae Applies to be an Astronaut, Then Something Awful Happens

Hi, it's Sneeze again.

In November 1985, Mae applied to NASA to enter the astronaut program. NASA stands for National Aeronautics and Space Administration, the people in charge of everything America does in space. If NASA accepted Mae, she would get to ride inside of a space shuttle and go into space, about 240 miles above the Earth, high enough to go into orbit. Going into orbit means you start circling around the Earth every 90 minutes.

On January 28, 1986, all seven astronauts inside the space shuttle called Challenger were killed only minutes after launch. When the Challenger launched, the booster engine failed and the shuttle broke apart. One of the astronauts was a school teacher.

I could tell that Mae was badly shaken up by this terrible thing. Would it change her mind about going into space? Well, if it did, who could blame her.

In 1987, NASA began plans to send a new shuttle into space. This shuttle was called Endeavour. I asked Mae why the new shuttle was named Endeavour. She said it was named for the British ship Endeavour that the explorer Captain James Cook took on his first voyage of discovery in 1770.

One cold, rainy evening in January 1987, a year after the Challenger explosion, Mae came home from her doctor job to the apartment we shared in Los Angeles. When I heard her key in the door, I greeted her as usual by jumping into her arms and licking her face with my scratchy, wet tongue.

She flopped onto the couch with her day's mail and started to look through it. When she found a large tan envelope, she got excited. She tore it open, read something, and screamed.

"Sneeze, do you know what this is?" she said.

"Tell me," I said.

"It's from NASA," she said excitedly. "They want me to update my application. They're looking for astronauts for the new space shuttle Endeavour!"

"Gracko!" I said. "Congratulations!"

I should have known that nothing on Earth could ever scare Mae out of going into space.   She stayed up late filling out forms and she mailed them the next morning on the way to work.

A few weeks later, she received a phone call at

her office, asking if she could come to the Johnson Space Center in Houston the following week for interviews and examinations. Out of the 2,000 people who applied for the shuttle Endeavour flight, NASA had narrowed that down to 100. After interviews and exams of those 100 people in Houston in the following week, Mae said they would narrow it down to 15 people. Then seven of those would be chosen as the crew for the Endeavour.

I have never seen Mae so pumped or so worried.

"Sneeze," she said, "how can I ask for a week off work at my doctor job on such short notice to go to Houston and try to become an astronaut? They're going to think I'm insane."

"Then why tell them the truth?" I asked.

She squeezed her eyes shut and shook her head.

"You know I could never lie to them like that," she said.

"Then how else could you lie to them?" I asked.

She stuck her tongue out at me.

"I know what I'll do," she said. "I'll go to Beverly, the office manager. She's really nice. I think she likes me, and I know she's a big fan of Star Trek on TV like I am. If she promises not to tell anybody, I think I can trust her with the truth."

I shrugged.

"That might work," I said. "But personally, I

recommend a big whopper of a lie."

Chapter 14

Houston, We Have a Problem

"So how did it go in Houston?" I asked Mae when she returned home and I finished licking her face.

"NASA gave me a week of tests," she said, wiping her face. "Written tests, eye tests, hearing tests, blood tests, strength tests, x-rays, and a complete physical exam. The FBI did a background check to make sure I wasn't a spy, a criminal, or someone with dangerous habits, like drinking too much liquor or using illegal drugs.

"They gave me a test to see if I was someone who freaks out in tight spaces," she said. "Astronauts have to spend a lot of time in very tight spaces. They had me climb into a balloon-like thing that was only three feet wide, which is pretty tight, and sit inside it with air blowing on me. Nobody told me how long I would have to sit there. It turned out to be only a half hour.

"I didn't have the slightest trouble spending a half hour in the balloon," she continued. "In fact, I hummed and sang to myself, and then I fell asleep. They had to wake me up. But when the flight surgeon listened to my heart through his stethoscope, he heard a whooshing, swishing sound, which told him that I probably had a heart murmur. A heart murmur is a noisy blood flow that could mean there was something wrong with my heart.

"I knew about my heart murmur from when I was in medical school. The doctor who examined me at medical school had said that my type of heart murmur wasn't a problem. And after several NASA doctors listened to my murmur, they all agreed."

Chapter 15

More News from NASA

When Mae returned from Houston to her office at CIGNA Health Plans, she told me everybody knew where she had been. They didn't think she was insane, as Mae expected. They were excited for her and they wanted her to tell them everything.

One night after she got home from CIGNA, she was really excited.

"Sneeze!" she screamed. "A man called me from NASA. He said, 'We wanted to know if you still wanted to be an astronaut.' 'Yes,' I said. 'Absolutely!' 'Well then, we'd like you to come on board,' he said. 'Thanks, Mae. Glad you're joining us.'

"Sneeze, we're moving to Houston! I did it! I'm going to be an astronaut!"

"Gracko!" I said. I licked her face.

She wiped her face, but she was grinning so widely her cheeks ached. She had finally achieved something she had wanted to do since she was 10 years old.

"The man from NASA said, 'Tomorrow at noon we will release a formal press notice announcing the names of everyone that's been selected, but please don't tell anybody until after that happens.'"

"You can't tell anybody?" I said. "Not even your sister, Ada Sue?"

"No," she said. "Not even Ada Sue. She couldn't keep a secret. The man at NASA said not to tell anybody until tomorrow after noon. How can I possibly keep my mouth shut that long? I better Krazy Glue my lips together."

Mae gave me a whole spoonful of catnip. Then she picked up the phone, called her parents, told them the news, and made them swear not to tell anybody.

Chapter 16

We Move to Houston Where Mae Will Train to Be an Astronaut

To become a NASA astronaut and go into space you have to train for at least two years. So Mae and I left Los Angeles and found a place to live in Houston, and Mae began her training to be a NASA astronaut.

Houston was different than other places Mae and I had lived before. Los Angeles and Chicago were both big cities that were hot and humid in summer, but Houston was hotter and more humid than I remember in both of those. People who lived in Houston had lots to tell me about it:

<u>WHAT FOLKS FROM HOUSTON TOLD ME ABOUT HOUSTON:</u>

<u>The weather:</u> If you expect it to be bad, it'll be bad. If you're a complainer, you'll have plenty to complain about.

<u>Summers:</u> During the summer, you wouldn't say Houston is hot and damp, you'd say it's like sitting in

a Turkish steam bath or walking through hot soup. If you go to Houston in summer, you pretty much have to stay underground—everything underground is air conditioned. All the buildings downtown are connected underground to air-conditioned restaurants, shops and other things. When it rains in Houston, which it does a lot, it's like standing under a waterfall.

<u>Flooding:</u> Bayous are like slow-moving swampy rivers. During hurricane season there's flooding from all four of Houston's bayous.

<u>Traffic:</u> There are lots of traffic jams in Houston, and many roads are just terrible. The traffic can be really bad. How bad? Like pull-your-hair-out-and-scream-at-the-road bad.

<u>Friendly:</u> People who live in Houston are very friendly, very helpful, very polite people —lots of pleases, thank-yous and where-y'all-froms.

<u>Mosquitoes:</u> The mosquitos in Houston are just plain awful.

<u>Not much to look at:</u> Houston doesn't have any beaches, any oceans, or any mountains, so there's really not very much to look at.

<u>How Houston stacks up against other cities:</u> Houston is the fourth biggest city in the US, right after New York, Los Angeles, and Chicago. Houston is the capital of space exploration, the capital of

air conditioning, and, according to Men's Fitness Magazine, the capital of people with the fattest bellies in the US. Now if you live in Houston and you have a fat belly, don't be mad at me or at Men's Fitness Magazine, just try eating less than three Big Macs every day at lunch. Most cats I know don't have big fat bellies. That's because most cats I know don't eat big Macs.

The Johnson Space Center: This is a group of buildings in Houston where NASA trains astronauts to fly in space shuttles to the International Space Station. You can visit some of these buildings and squeeze into space shuttles that used to be in space, but that NASA isn't using anymore. You can also squeeze into exact models of things that are still in space.

If you go to the Johnson Space Center, you should allow about six hours. You'll see the Saturn 5 Rocket, Mission Control, and the Neutral Buoyancy Lab pool in which they keep an exact model of the International Space Station. That's where astronauts in underwater spacesuits learn how it will feel to do spacewalks on the real International Space Station. (More about that later.)

You will probably meet a few real astronauts in the Johnson Space Center. Or their cats. Wouldn't that be cool? Meeting a real astronaut like Mae

Jemison would be almost as cool as being an astronaut yourself and blasting into outer space. And a whole lot safer. (Actually, you'd have a lot better chance of meeting an astronaut than meeting one of their cats.)

Chapter 17

Mae Begins Her Astronaut Training

Some of Mae's astronaut training was really scary. I heard that one of the things they make you do was to throw you out of a two-seat jet plane going 750 miles per hour. That sounded too dangerous for anybody to do, much less a cat like me.

One day Mae came back from training early and made herself a cup of tea. Seemed like this might be a good time to ask her some questions for my bio. I hopped up on the arm of our sofa, made a point of not digging my claws into it as I sometimes do, and started.

"Mae," I said, "is it true that part of astronaut training is to get thrown out of a jet plane going 750 miles per hour?"

"Yep."

"How could you do that?" I asked. "And why would you want to?"

fire and it was about to explode, I might not want to remain on board. So I would pull a lever on the side of my seat. The rockets under my butt would first blow off the clear plastic canopy over my head. Then they'd blow me and the seat I was sitting on out of the cockpit. After I'm blown out of the plane, my seat would fall away from me, and the parachute on my backpack would open automatically. Within a few seconds, I'd be floating over the plane with my parachute fluttering over my head. Then I would then float to the ground or into the ocean below me, hopefully at a speed that wouldn't kill me."

"Yowr!" I said. "That sounds awful. Did you actually have to do that?"

"Not yet," she said. "So far they just put me on the deck of a boat in the ocean with a parachute strapped to my back. Then they had a helicopter swoop down, hook onto my parachute harness, yank me off the boat, pull me a few hundred feet into the air and let me go. When my parachute opened, I floated slowly down and plopped into the freezing water of the ocean."

"Wasn't that scary?" I asked.

"Of course," she said. "Also wet and teeth-chatteringly cold. But better than being exploded out of a plane going 750 miles per hour. When you do that, I hear the pressure of your harness straps will bruise your shoulders, and it might even break your collarbone."

"Oh, wow," I said. "Are there any more things like that?"

"Well, there's one thing where they fly us in a plane that climbs into the air and then suddenly plunges downward."

"Uh-oh."

"Actually," she said, "I hear that that one is kind of fun. To get astronauts used to the weightlessness of things in space, they take us for rides in a big, empty airplane, a KC-135. A typical flight lasts two to three hours. The plane climbs into the air, then it suddenly plunges downward in 20- to 25-second dips, like a big roller coaster.

"That gives us the feeling of the weightlessness in space," she said. "Most astronauts call this plane the Vomit Comet. Even experienced astronauts who have been in space get sick on the Vomit Comet. They train astronauts to get used to spacewalks, where they have to climb out of the shuttle and fix things," she said.

"Climbing out of a shuttle sounds really dangerous," I said.

"You bet," she said.

"What keeps you from floating away into space forever?"

"Well, when you're doing a spacewalk," she said, "you're attached to the shuttle by a long cable called a tether."

"And that makes it safe?" I said.

"No, it's still very dangerous," she said. "What's also dangerous is that in space there's no air for you to breathe. And the temperature in the daytime is as high as 275 degrees, and as cold as minus 250 degrees."

"But your spacesuit protects you from all that, right?" I said.

"Not your orange spacesuit, which you wear when you're in the shuttle during liftoff and when you head back toward Earth," she said. "Astronauts call it a pumpkin suit because it's bright orange like a pumpkin. The orange spacesuit has tubes of water running through it to keep you at a safe and comfortable temperature. In case your supply of oxygen runs out, the orange suit has an emergency supply. The orange suit takes about 10 minutes to put on, and it weighs 30 pounds."

"That's three times as heavy as a cat like me,"

I said. "Do you wear your orange spacesuit on spacewalks outside the shuttle?"

"No," she said. "Outside the shuttle we would have to wear a special white spacesuit that has its own air supply. The reason it's white is because white reflects heat in space the same as it does on Earth. The white suit has its own ability to keep us comfortable, no matter how baking hot or below-freezing cold it is in outer space. It takes 45 minutes to put on a white spacesuit. When it's worn in space, it weighs nothing at all. On Earth, it weighs 280 pounds with nobody inside of it."

"That's as heavy as 28 cats my size standing close together," I said.

"Another way they train us for weightless spacewalks besides the Vomit Comet," Mae said, "is in a gigantic indoor swimming pool called the Neutral Buoyancy Laboratory. We call it NBL for short. Neutral Buoyancy is just a fancy way of saying that when you're in a swimming pool, you're floating and you're weightless, just like when you're in deep space. The NBL pool is 40 feet deep, and it holds over six million gallons of water. That's about seven times deeper than an Olympic-sized pool, and over nine times more water. At the bottom of the pool is an exact full-sized model of the International Space Station."

"What's the International Space Station?" I asked.

"It's a laboratory that's been in space, in orbit around the Earth, since the year 2000," she said. "Astronauts from 15 countries have spent time there. That's why they call it international. It's the largest man-made thing in space. It's as long as a football field. It travels 17,500 miles per hour, and it circles the Earth like a very small moon about 15 times every day. It cost about 150 billion dollars. I heard that it's the most expensive thing ever built."

"Could I see the Space Station from Earth if I knew where to look?" I asked.

"If you knew where to look," she said, "you might. It would look like a tiny point of light."

"How high up is it?" I asked.

"About 240 miles," she said.

"What's it like inside the Space Station?"

"It has two bathrooms, a gym and more rooms than a six-bedroom house," she said.

"Then what is it doing at the bottom of a giant swimming pool?" I asked.

Mae smiled.

"First of all," she said, "remember that the Space Station at the bottom of the giant swimming pool is only a full-sized model of the real one. It was made to train us to be able to fix things outside the shuttle on spacewalks. When we put on our bulky white spacesuits, jump into the pool and go underwater to fix something on the Space Station, it will feel like we're actually on a spacewalk fixing the real Space Station. We spend a lot of time under water. Sometimes we stay under for seven hours at a time. That way we get used to the feeling of being weightless, because we'll feel weightless all the time in space."

"Glub!" I said. "Most of us cats—including me—don't like water. The only time I ever got wet was when I fell into your bathtub. I smelled like lavender soap for three days. Yuck! And the only time I felt weightless was when I was falling out of a high window in Sierra Leone before you rescued me. That was scary but it was kind of fun, too. And I didn't get hurt."

Mae smiled. "Weightlessness is kind of fun, once you get used to it," she said, "but it's not great for your body to be weightless for a long time. If your body doesn't have to do the work of carrying your weight around, your muscles can get weak and your bones, too.

"The most important muscle in the human body is the heart," she said. "In space, our hearts don't pump as much blood as they do on Earth, because they don't have as much work to do. So we have to find other ways to give our hearts more work. On

the Endeavour, a stationary bicycle was a good way
to make our hearts do some extra work to keep them
strong."

"I read on the NASA website that, in their first
year of training, astronauts have to go to survival
school," I said. "They take six or seven astronauts
into wild places like the woods or the desert and
leave them there for lots of days with no food, no
water, and no directions. Cats can go a long time
without food or water. I did it a lot before you found
me. It wasn't that terrible. But from what I know
about humans, this would be awfully hard for them.
I don't see why they have to do it."

"It may sound kind of strange," said Mae. "But
the reason they do it is that, in our first year of
training, we'll be flying on Earth-based training
planes. What if one of these planes crashes on
a mountain, or in the desert, or in the ocean? If
that happens, we have to know how to survive
by ourselves for a while. So they teach us how to
build a fire without matches, how to build a shelter
from rain or snow or heat, how to handle medical
emergencies, and so on.

"They may drop us off in a freezing, snowy place
in Canada for a week," she said, "or plop us on a raft
in the ocean for a few days. They teach us how to
find drinkable water, and how to make undrinkable

water drinkable. They teach us how to tell which plant leaves or roots—or even beetles—we can eat without being poisoned."

"Beetles?" I said. "Yuck! I ate a beetle once and threw up two minutes later. You should tell your astronauts that squeek-squeeks—mice—are yummy, and good for you, too."

Mae rolled her eyes. "Only if you're a cat," she said.

Chapter 18

What Would It Feel Like to Be on a Space Shuttle Launch?

I, Sneeze, haven't flown in space myself because I'm a cat, and cats aren't allowed on space shuttles. And even flying on a regular airplane always makes me want to throw up a hairball.

But a good writer always tries to give the reader an experience, so I want you to feel what it would be like to be getting ready to launch in the space shuttle. Mae told me a lot about what happened when she launched into space. And I read whatever true space stuff I could get my paws on, including a really good book called Spaceman, written by another astronaut, Mike Massamino, so I'm pretty sure the following is very close to what you'd feel like.

I'd like to say, "Close your eyes and imagine this is your day to go into space," but you'll need to keep your eyes open to read this. I'm sure you're smart enough to imagine things even with your eyes open. Here goes:

You've squished yourself into your 30-pound orange spacesuit way before the sun comes up and you ride out to the launch pad before dawn. It's totally dark outside and the birdies are still snoring in their nests.

Now you walk toward the tower in which you'll take the elevator up to the entrance of the shuttle. You're carrying your large, round helmet, which will snap into the collar of your pumpkin suit and then lock into place. The front of your helmet has a big clear plastic visor that you can slide open whenever you're in a place that has air you can breathe.

Very bright lights make the space shuttle glow in the dark. The shuttle looks like a rocket-shaped baby airliner with swept-back wings, standing with its pointy nose sticking straight up. Attached to the shuttle are what looks like two shorter, white, pointy-nosed rocket boosters. Also attached to the shuttle is a taller, fatter, brown-colored, cylindrieal, pointy-nosed fuel tank. It's as tall as a 15-storey building.

Mae says the group of four pointy-nosed things is called a stack, and it looks like something you'd see at Disneyland. The tallest, fattest fuel tank holds more than a million and a half pounds of highly explosive rocket fuel. This tank doesn't get filled until shortly before lift-off, because filling it turns it into a gigantic bomb.

You hear the eerie sounds coming from the shuttle —hissing steam, metal groaning as the below-zero cold of the rocket fuel hits the sides of the tank. Enormous clouds of steam rise into the sky. The strangeness of the strange sounds and sights in the dark gives you a shiver of excitement— and fear.

You get on the elevator in the tower that takes you up to the launch platform 90 feet above you. And there's a bathroom at the top! Probably a good idea to stop for a pee here in what astronauts call The Last Toilet on Earth.

The ground crew now guides you and the astronaut crew across the passageway between the tower and the shuttle. You find yourself in a small room where they strap a harness onto your back with a heavy survival pack. It's heavier than hauling six cats my size on your back. Inside your survival pack is a parachute.

Wait—a parachute? What good is a parachute if you're on a shuttle that's being blasted into space 240 miles above the Earth? If something goes wrong, do they expect you to jump out of the space shuttle and parachute down 240 miles? —

Now the ground crew leads you through the open hatch to the windowless mid-deck of the shuttle. Up a short ladder is the flight deck, but at least the flight deck has windows. Four astronauts in orange spacesuits, including the commander and the pilot, have been strapped into their chairs on the flight deck, which have been tilted upwards for the launch. They're all lying on their backs with their legs up. That's the best position for take-off and the first part of the flight.

The astronauts wave to you from their chairs. They seem surprised to see someone your age on the shuttle who isn't an astronaut.

"So how do you like it so far?" one of them asks you.

Frankly, so far there hasn't been much to like.

"It's really cool," you say because you're too polite to tell them the truth.

"Bet you can't wait to tell all your friends about this," says one of the astronauts.

You want to say, "Yeah, assuming I don't get blown to pieces," but you don't because they might not think it was funny. You yourself don't think it was funny. In fact, you're starting to worry that the million and a half gallons of explosive rocket fuel in the tallest, fattest tank that's attached to your shuttle really could blow you to pieces.

The ground crew leads you back down the ladder to the mid-deck for the launch. Three more astronauts are strapped into seats in the mid-deck. They're flying on their backs, too, with their legs up.

The ground crew straps you tightly into your seat and snaps your helmet into the collar ring on your pumpkin suit and then locks it in place. Breathing in your helmet makes you sound like Darth Vader. The ground crew checks the flow of oxygen inside your helmet to make sure you'll get enough to breathe when you're in space. And then they leave you.

Now you lie there, listening to the countdown to liftoff. The launch could be canceled right up till the very last second if something isn't exactly right. Nothing is more important than keeping the astronauts safe.

The countdown actually started almost two days ago, 43 hours before the planned launch. At every step along the way to zero and launch, equipment and systems are checked and checked again.

Since there's nothing to do till launch, your eyes wander to the emergency and safety signs on the walls. They say what to do and where to go in an emergency. One of the astronauts watches you reading the signs.

"Something to read before you die," he says with what sounds like a chuckle.

You think he's kidding, but you aren't sure, so you don't laugh.

The countdown has been going on for hours. Now, a few seconds before launch, some of the engines start up. In the next few seconds, one of three things will happen: (1) the space shuttle you're on will blast through the Earth's atmosphere at 17,500 miles per hour, or (2) the flight might be canceled, or (3) the shuttle could explode. All of these things have happened on shuttles.

The countdown is now T-minus-6-seconds, which means 6 seconds till blast-off. The shuttle's three main engines roar into life. You don't just hear it, you can feel it in every part of your body. You lie on your back, listening to the engines. The spacecraft shudders and shakes, getting ready to break away from the Earth. As astronaut Mike Massimino says, it feels like a giant dog has grabbed the shuttle in his jaws and he's shaking it back and forth like a chew toy.

At the count of T-minus-0-seconds, the two white solid rocket boosters on each side of your shuttle are turned on, and the bolts that anchor the Endeavour to the ground are shattered by small explosions. The shuttle tilts forward. Then it tilts back upright. And then it blasts into the sky.

As the shuttle rises, you feel like a pile of concrete blocks has landed on your chest. If you weigh 100 pounds on Earth, you actually weigh 300 pounds right now! That's because as the speed of the shuttle increases, the effect of gravity increases. At this point in the flight, gravity has three times as much effect on you as it does on Earth.

The shuttle goes from zero to 17,500 miles an hour in eight-and-a-half minutes—that's eight-and-a-half minutes to get 240 miles above the Earth and into orbit! The color of the sky had gone from light blue, to dark blue, to black.

At 70 miles up, the shuttle breaks through the Earth's atmosphere. You hear two muffled explosions outside the shuttle —Fump! Fump! The bolts attaching the tallest, fattest fuel tank to the

shuttle were just blown off. You are 70 miles above
the Earth. The tallest, fattest fuel tank has fallen off.

Wait—what? The fuel tank has fallen off?

Yes, but don't worry, that's what it was supposed
to do. It was completely empty, and no longer
needed. By the time it tumbles back through the
Earth's atmosphere again, it will get so hot it breaks
into small pieces that fall into the ocean.

Suddenly, the shuttle engines stop. The shuddering and the roaring has stopped. It feels like you're sitting straight up, but you're not. You're still strapped flat on your back. It's strangely quiet. Now there's only the soft sound of the engine's cooling fans. It's like the purring of many happy cats.

Although it felt like you came to a complete stop when the engines were turned off, you are actually still traveling at 17,500 miles an hour!

How can that be possible? I have no idea, because I'm only a cat. But I'll tell you what Mae told me. Your inner ear responds to gravity. With no gravity signals coming in, your inner ear thinks you're not moving anymore. So your inner ear is stupid. That's not what Mae said, but that's what I, Sneeze the cat, am saying.

The astronaut sitting ahead of you turns around to speak.

"You can take off your helmet now," he says to you.

Is he kidding, or is he playing a nasty trick on you to show you there's no breathable air in the shuttle now? You notice that he still has his own helmet on.

"Why should I take my helmet off?" you ask.

"Because I want to show you something," he answers.

The other two astronauts are looking at you and

grinning. Would these astronauts be grinning at you if they thought that taking off your helmet would make it impossible for you to breathe? No, of course not! Not if you know anything about astronauts. So you take off your helmet and hold it. You're relieved to find that you can still breathe as well as you could inside your helmet before the launch.

"Now let your helmet fall," says the astronaut who told you to take it off.

You shrug and let your helmet fall. But it doesn't fall. It just floats in front of you. Weightless. Your face shows how amazed you are. How on earth can this be possible? Because we're not on Earth, that's how.

All three astronauts burst out laughing.

"Congratulations," says your new astronaut friend. "You are now in space. You are now in orbit. And you made it without blowing up! You are now an honorary astronaut!"

Everybody cheers. Including you.

CHAPTER 19

Mae Boards the Space Shuttle Endeavour

Mae reported to NASA in Houston in August 1992. I rode with Mae and a friend of hers on a NASA bus to the Kennedy Space Center launch site to see her blast into space on the Endeavour.

The Endeavour had already been attached to the huge brown external rocket. When we were pretending that you, the reader, were going on a ride on a shuttle, I had thought the shuttle looked like a chubby baby airliner on the back of a mommy airliner. Now it looked more like a fly on a can of soda.

The Endeavour's ground crew led Mae into the elevator of the structure that took astronauts up to the shuttle's entrance.

"Per muffer!" I called out to her, which meant 'Good luck!' in Cattish. Then I got on a NASA bus with Mae's friend and we rode to the viewing stands six miles away. The shuttle finally blasted off with a chest-rattling rumble. We stood there watching the launch on the TV screens, holding our breaths till the shuttle was out of sight and we knew Mae was safe.

Mae spent eight days, from September 12 to 20 in 1992, on the Endeavor space shuttle. With her were five other NASA American astronauts and the first Japanese astronaut, Dr. Mohri Mamoru. The international crew was divided into two teams for around-the-clock operations.

Mae's job during this mission was to do experiments on herself and on the other astronauts to study why humans get motion sickness in space, and how space flight causes changes in bone cell function and become weaker during space flight. She also studied whether frog tadpoles can develop without gravity.

Mae began each of her work shifts with the words "Hailing frequencies open," which any fan of the old Star Trek TV show would recognize from what Lieutenant Uhura always said.

"Since I came back to Earth," Mae said to me a few weeks after she returned, "people ask me, 'What was it like to fly on the Endeavour?'"

"What do you tell them?" I asked.

"I smile and ask, 'What part do you want to hear about? The launch itself? My job on the space shuttle? Floating in space?""

"Yeah," I said. "How could you even describe floating in space to someone who has never done it?"

"Well," she said, "I tell them it's fun—which it is. You have incredible leaping abilities and hang-time in space, but it does take some getting used to. I tell them you can float, but you have to stay close to a wall so you can push off from it in the direction you want to go instead of just hanging helplessly in the air."

"What do you tell them Earth looks like from space?" I asked.

"I say it looks like a huge blue marble floating in the blackness of space," she said. "I was surprised by how blue it looked, about how much of it was water. Our Earth is three-quarters water and it looks like it from space. When you're in orbit, it seems you're always over the bright blue Pacific Ocean.

"There are actually some people who really believe that the Earth is flat, not round," she said. "They proudly call themselves Flat Earthers. I wish they could all see the Earth from space. It couldn't possibly be any rounder. The Flat Earthers wouldn't have any choice but to join the Round Earthers."-

"If the Earth was flat," I said, "cats would have found the edge and pushed everything off of it by now."

Mae laughed and applauded.

"What does the moon look like from space?" I asked.

"From Earth, the moon looks like a flat white disc," she said. "From space it looks like a big, three-dimensional ball. Like a big gray planet. You can even make out some of the craters and mountains on the moon's surface."

"You can see the craters on the moon through a telescope on Earth," I said.

"You're right," she said.

"What did the stars look like when you were in space?" I asked.

"When you look through the shuttle's windows during nighttime," she said, "stars look like very bright pinpoints of light. When we see stars from Earth, they seem to flicker—they get brighter and dimmer. That's because the light from the stars has to travel through the Earth's atmosphere before we see it, and the atmosphere is always changing. If the atmosphere is a bit thicker, starlight travels a little slower. If the atmosphere is a bit thinner, starlight travels a little faster. And in space, we see that stars come in many colors. Not just white."

I twitched my tail from side to side—that's the way we cats show we're interested. Mae knows me well enough to know this. She continued.

"When you're in space," she said, "you see stars that are red, blue, yellow, or other colors. The colors tell us how hot they are. The color of a star depends on its surface temperature. The hotter the star, the shorter the wavelength of light it will give off. The hottest ones are blue or blue-white, which are shorter wavelengths of light. Cooler stars are red or red-brown, which have longer wavelengths.

"The yellow stars like our sun, which are among the cooler ones, might have planets that have life on them like ours. By the way, I'm sure you'll like this— stars smell like steak!"

Now my tail twitched and my eyes widened. I was really interested—and getting hungry, too.

"When stars start to burn out, they give off a smell like burnt steak," she said.

"How far away are we from our nearest star?" I asked.

"Well," she said, "our nearest star is Alpha Centauri. It's a little more than four light years away from Earth."

"What does 'four light years' mean?" I asked.

"A light year means how far light can travel in one year. Light travels faster than we humans can even imagine—almost 6 trillion miles in one year. That's 670-million miles per hour. More than

186-thousand miles per second. If we could travel at the speed of light, we could race around our Earth seven-and-a-half times in just one second!"

"So the light we see from Alpha Centauri today left that star four years ago," I said. "And how many miles did it travel in four years?"

Mae did some figuring on an envelope.

"Twenty-four trillion miles," she said.

"And a trillion is three million, right?" I asked.

Mae laughed and shook her head.

"No, Sneeze," she said, "a trillion is one thousand billion," she said. "We can't see how Alpha Centauri looks now, we can only see it the way it looked four years ago. If Alpha Centauri died and disappeared three years ago, we would still see it today because its light would still be arriving on Earth. Most stars we see are much farther away than Alpha Centauri. Some of them are so far away that their light doesn't reach us for thousands or even millions of years. So we may be seeing some stars that died thousands or even millions of years ago!"

"Mae, I just don't get how it could take thousands or millions of years for light to travel to us," I said. "How many light years away is our sun?"

"Do you remember I told you that when I was a little girl, my Uncle Louis would point up at the night sky and say that the stars were all suns that were very far away?" she said. "Well, our sun is definitely a star, but it's not light years away like Alpha Centauri. It's only 93-million miles away from Earth."

"Only 93-million miles away from Earth?" I said. "Compared to the other stars, that seems like a walk around the block."

"You know how long it takes light from our sun to reach us on Earth?" asked Mae.

"How long?" I said.

"Eight minutes," Mae said.

Discussions with big numbers are tiring for cats, even cats who are members of The Feline Historical Society. I need to take a short cat nap before I continue.

Before I take my short cat nap, I have to see if you can answer an amazing question Mae just asked me. Ready? OK Here we go: How much bigger is the planet Jupiter than our planet Earth? Is Jupiter 4 times as big as Earth? 20 times as big as Earth? Or 100 times as big as Earth?

I'll bet you never guessed the answer: Jupiter is more than 1,300 times as big as Earth! That means more than 1,300 of our Earths could fit inside of Jupiter! Try that on your friends._

Chapter 20

How Astronauts Poop in Space and Do Other Stuff

I'm always interested in the differences between how cats and humans do simple everyday things. And I'm also really interested in differences between how humans do things on Earth and how they do them in space. So that's partly what this chapter is about.

When we cats live outside, we poop in the dirt and then cover it up so the smell doesn't attract another animal who wants to eat us. When we live inside with our humans, we just hop into the litter box.

On Earth, humans poop in a toilet that flushes everything away. In space, pooping is a lot more complicated. I didn't feel super comfortable asking Mae about this, so first I read a lot of NASA articles about pooping in space. This is what I found out:

On NASA's missions during the 1960s, the only equipment they had for astronauts to poop in space was plastic bags that they taped to their butts.

The toilet on the International Space Station has a seat like toilets on Earth, but it's just about impossible to actually sit on it when you're weightless and floating around. Most astronauts float directly over it and try to poop into the small target hole underneath them. The turds that miss their target float above the toilet and have to be caught before they fly away. Or smack you in the face.

Apollo 10's mission in 1969 was practice for a moon landing, so that the next mission, Apollo 11, would know exactly how to land two astronauts on the moon. Halfway through Apollo 10's eight-day mission, they realized they had a poop problem.

Here is the actual conversation from the Apollo 10 onboard tape recorder. The voices are the three astronauts that were on Apollo 10—Pilot Gene Cernan, Commander Tom Stafford, and Pilot John Young. Their conversation begins when they first discover that they have the problem:

STAFFORD: Give me a napkin quick. There's a turd floating through the air!

YOUNG: I didn't do it. It ain't one of mine.

CERNAN: I don't think it's one of mine.

STAFFORD: Mine was a little more sticky than that. Throw that away.

CERNAN: No more turds are going to fit in

there (meaning the waste compartment).

Not sure what happened after that, but in space when floating turds are caught, they're usually put into plastic bags and pushed down into solid waste containers. These are released into space every 10 days. Sometimes the poop burns up and sometimes it explodes.

Breaking a toilet in space is a lot more expensive than breaking one on Earth. I read a NASA report that said when the only toilet on the International Space Station broke in 2008, NASA had to replace it with one from Russia. You know what it cost them? Nineteen million dollars!

I asked Mae, who was reading an engineering manual at the time, if she could guess how much it cost NASA to replace a broken toilet on the International Space Station.

"Nineteen million dollars," she said without looking up.

"Uh, right," I said. I was a little annoyed that she had known the exact amount, but I wasn't surprised. "Mae, you know how NASA could save a fortune on space toilets?"

"No, Sneeze," she said with a sigh because she was trying to concentrate on what she was reading. "How could NASA save a fortune on space toilets?"

"By replacing them with human-sized litter

boxes," I said.

"Uh . . . right," she said without turning around and telling me what a great idea I had.

"I was thinking that, since they love you over at NASA," I said, "maybe you could tell them my idea."

"I don't think they'd be interested, Sneeze," she said, still reading her engineering manual.

"Well, they might be if you said it was your idea, not your cat's," I said, feeling a little
hurt.

"The problem isn't whose idea it was," Mae said.

"Really?" I said. "Well, I think that even you would have liked that idea if you'd heard it from one of your astronaut buddies instead of from a cat."

She turned around and looked at me.

"Sneeze, " she said gently, "you're a wonderful cat and I love you dearly. But human litter boxes in space just isn't a good idea. It's clear you haven't quite grasped the idea of gravity yet. Whatever a human left in the litter box wouldn't stay there. It would just float near it. But you're a cat and you didn't realize that, and that's fine. I'm sorry, sweetheart."

All right, whatever. I read that when NASA's six Apollo missions visited the moon, they left behind a total of 96 huge bags of poop. And those bags are still there on the moon. If extra-terrestrial creatures ever found them, wouldn't it be fun to ask what they thought was in the bags and what it was doing there?

Peeing in space: Astronauts—both men and women—can pee into a long tube with a vacuum system that sucks it away. Space toilets on board the International Space Station collect astronaut pee—then nearly all of it gets filtered and recycled, and it becomes drinking water for the astronauts! Yuck!

Actually, the filtered and recycled pee is actually purer than the water that comes out of the kitchen sink faucets in most North American homes, and it tastes like . . . water.

Russian astronauts riding in the bus that takes them to the launch pad of their space shuttle always ask the bus driver to stop. (In Russia, their astronauts are called cosmonauts.) The men get off the bus and, for good luck, they pee on the back wheel of the bus on the right side. The women pee into a cup and splash it on the wheel. They do this to honor Russian cosmonaut Yuri Gagarin, the first human who had to pee on the way to his first launch in 1961. Speaking of peeing in space, I must tell you something I just read in a NASA publication: "Neil Armstrong was the first man to walk on the moon, but Buzz Aldrin was the first man to pee on it."

Peeing or pooping during a spacewalk: An astronaut in a white spacesuit who works outside of the shuttle for hours where there aren't any toilets must wear a very large diaper, like a grown-up baby. When the spacewalk is over, the astronaut takes off the diaper and gets dressed in regular work clothes.

<u>Farting in space:</u> On Earth, farts are stinky, but they're not dangerous. But if you're an astronaut in the tiny cabin of a space shuttle in outer space, a fart can quickly become a problem because it has nowhere to go, so it just hangs there. And some of the gases in farts are flammable, which means that they can catch fire or even explode!

<u>Sleeping in space:</u> OK, sleeping in space isn't gross or funny like pooping, peeing or farting in space, but it's still kind of interesting. Sleeping in space is different than sleeping on Earth. Everything is weightless in space, so astronauts either lie down or stand up to sleep in sleeping bags that they clip to the ceiling or to a wall. That's so they don't float around and smack their heads.

NASA found that, even if astronauts are floating, they like to sleep with their heads on pillows, so NASA designed pillows that astronauts attach to their heads with headbands.

On the International Space Station, astronauts sleep in soundproof booths where they can listen to music, use a laptop, and store personal things in nets attached to the cabin walls. Every 24 hours on the

International Space Station, there are 16 sunrises and 16 sunsets, so it's hard to know when it's time to go to bed. To keep out the sunlight, astronauts either pull shutters over the windows or they cover their eyes with eyeshades.

Eating in space: You don't have to cook in space because your entire food supply is prepared and packed in foil pouches before you blast off on the shuttle. Most of the food is dehydrated, which means that the water was taken out of it. So before you eat it, you have to open the pouch and add water to it. If you want to heat it, there are ovens in shuttles and the International Space Station.

Here are some things that astronauts eat in space: Macaroni and cheese, spaghetti and meatballs, shrimp, lasagna, and steak. Yum.

Well, if you're reading this, you're probably a human, so you would probably think "Yum" for mac and cheese and steak and lasagna. I, being a cat, would think "Yum" for a nice juicy mouse, or as we call it in Cattish, a squeek-squeek. Sure, go ahead and say "Yuck" about eating a mouse. But don't knock it till you've tried it.

In space, you have to be careful while you eat, because all your food floats. And it will try to get away from you, which means you'll have to chase it. Uh-oh, watch out, two of your meatballs are trying to get away!

In space, astronauts don't eat bread because it crumbles. If bread crumbs float around inside the spacecraft, astronauts could snuffle them inside their nose. So in space you shouldn't eat a peanut butter and jelly sandwich. But if you don't mind peanut butter and jelly without the bread, that would be all right.

<u>Being weightless in space:</u> If you think being weightless in space is fun, you're right. You can float several feet off the floor without even trying. You can push off a wall and fly through a room. You can imagine you're Superman or Wonder Woman.

And if you think that being weightless in space could be a pain in the butt, you're right, too. For example: Until you get used to weightlessness, whenever you reach for something and try to pick it up, you will probably bat it away from you. Then you'll have to chase it to get it back. When you float through a room, you'll probably smack your head. In space you're like a baby learning how to use your hands and feet all over again. You need to learn how to do the most ordinary things in a new way. —

Also in space, if you spin around, you won't feel that it's you who's spinning around. You'll feel it's the room that's spinning around, and that will make you feel like barfing. And the more you move about, the more you'll feel like puking your guts out. Hey, doesn't that sound like fun?

Chapter 21

What Does Chicago Look Like from Space?

"Mae," I said, "can you tell me what it was like to see Chicago from space?"

"Sure, Sneeze," she said. "Shortly after liftoff, I was in the shuttle's mid-deck. They were folding and putting away our orange launch suits and turning it into a space lab. Over my headphones I heard the voice of our mission commander say, 'Mae, please come up to the flight deck.'

"I floated up through the open hatch between the mid-deck and the flight deck. The commander pointed downward out of the flight deck windows. 'Chicago is about to come up, Mae,' he said.

"I looked where he was pointing," she said. "About 240 miles below us, my hometown, Chicago, slowly slid into view. The gray concrete of the streets, sidewalks, and buildings made the city look gray against the green of the farmland that surrounded it. I knew that in a building 240 miles below me were my parents.

"It was such a significant moment," she said. "I remembered being the little girl down there in the 1960s, when the only astronauts in space were men. That little girl wanted so powerfully to be up here where I was now. And I had managed to fulfill her dream. As I watched Chicago slide slowly out of sight, I thought if that little girl could have seen her older self now, she would have had a huge grin on her face."

CHAPTER 22

The First Real Astronaut on Star Trek

In 1993, a new character appeared in an episode of Star Trek, a popular TV show about the crew of the starship USS Enterprise and its missions in space in the 23rd century. The new character's name was Lieutenant Palmer, and she was a tall human from Earth. She had brown skin and an unusual short hairdo.

She wasn't an actor like everyone else in the cast. She was my friend and roommate, Mae Jemison, the first real astronaut who had actually been in orbit in space, circling the Earth at the speed of 17,500 miles an hour. She fulfilled two dreams she'd had when she was 10 years old. One was to be in space with other astronauts. The other was to be on Star Trek with her idol, Lieutenant Uhura.

"I always knew I would go into space someday," Mae told me. "But I secretly dreamed that someday I would play a part on TV with Lieutenant Uhura on an episode of Star Trek."

Well, folks, Mae was right. Who says you can't fulfill your wildest dreams?

All you have to do is be incredibly smart, work incredibly hard, be incredibly brave, have incredibly supportive parents, graduate high school and college and medical school with honors, become an engineer and a doctor, save the lives of people in developing countries, go through exhausting and terrifying astronaut training, and risk being blown to bits in a space shuttle.

That's all there is to it. Nothing too hard to do there, folks. A piece of cake, really. Amazing that so few ever manage to pull it off. Could I, a cat named Sneeze, have done it myself? I honestly don't know. Maybe. Probably. But if I had an opposable thumb on each paw? Then almost certainly.

CHAPTER 23

Since Mae Came Back from Space, Has She Found Anything to Do?

When Mae returned from space, she was famous. She was voted into the National Women's Hall of Fame. People Magazine voted her one of the 50 Most Beautiful People in the World. She was asked to be a guest or a host on TV news programs, and she was in TV commercials. She was invited to be on the Board of Directors of the World Sickle-Cell Foundation. Remember all this started when her mother asked her to find out what sickle cell anemia was? And now she's on the Board of Directors of the World Sickle-Cell Foundation? Not too bad, huh?

Mae decided it was time to leave NASA, so she said goodbye and she started a group of international science camps called The Earth We Share. The camps began as four-week sleep-away programs for girls and boys age 12 to 16, but now they also have day camps and one-week, non-sleep-over summer programs. Students come from around the world to learn problem-solving skills in science. The camp is free to qualified applicants.

She also became a professor of Environmental Studies at Dartmouth College.

She also created the Jemison Group, which develops science and technology companies.

She also created BioSentient Corporation, a medical equipment and medical services company.

She also created the Dorothy Jemison Foundation for Excellence, which designs educational programs to teach Science, Technology, Engineering, and Math.

She also created the 100 Year Starship Project. Their goal is to able humans to travel beyond our own solar system to another one during the next 100 years. NASA thought this was such a great idea that they put their money where their mouth is. So did The Defense Advanced Research Projects Agency, which is a part of the US Department of Defense that develops new weapons for our military.

Other than that, Mae is, you know, just kind of catching up on her reading, her writing, her lecturing, creating new science-related companies and stuff like that.

CHAPTER 24

A Visit from Wolfie

I was nervous when I opened the door of our Houston apartment and saw who had come to see me. A large female cat with long gray fur and a tail as fluffy as a fox walked inside as if she owned the place.

"Hello, Wolfie," I said. "I hope you didn't have any trouble finding the place."

"I don't have trouble finding places, Sneeze," she said, looking around our living room as if she wasn't impressed. "How long have you and Dr. Jemison been living here?"

"About two years," I said.

She nodded. "Pity you didn't have more time to fix it up," she said.

"Uh, right," I said. "So how did you like the first draft of my Jemison bio?"

"Well, the material about Dr. Jemison's early life was interesting," she said. "And I found the material about space travel fascinating. And I agree with your chapter of things you don't like that people say about cats, and your chapter proving cats are better than dogs, but I'm not sure that they have a place in a biography of Dr. Jemison . . ."

"Uh huh . . ."

"And I haven't the slightest idea why you thought a chapter that tells how male hippopotamuses use poop to attract a female to make babies, or the chapter about how to say 'Where is the toilet?' in the Krio language, or the chapter about how to go to the litter box in space where there's no gravity and your poop can smack you in the face—why you thought any of those chapters have a place in a biography of the first woman of color to go into deep space."

"Uh huh," I said. "But otherwise you liked it?"

"Sneeze," she said, "we have a lot of work to do before I can show it to the Feline Historical Society."

"Uh huh," I said. "Well, I'm glad you liked at least a few of the parts."

Cattish Vocabulary

Browr: Wants
Croo: Or
Crow: Just
Fffft: Mad
Fffft-fffft: Insults
Flurr: To do with
Foofy: No, seriously
Frau: Family
Froom: Work
Gracko: Congratulations
Laurel: Anything
Lore: To speak
Lum-lum: Lap-cat
Mee: You
Meer: Who
Meer browr merff?: Who wants to know?
Mel: Can
Meow: Hello, goodbye or peace

Merff: To know
Merl: This
Merow: Be sure
Mowi: Do you
Mowr: I was
Muffer: Luck
Per: Good
Per muffer: Good luck
Pert: Me
Prim: Really
Prowl: I'm better
Rare: Feeling upset
Rilff: Without
Row: How
Rowl: Have
Snap: Trap
Squeek-squeek: Mouse
Yaw: Feed me NOW
Yawoo: Scares
Yowr: That's scary

Sources

A Partial Bibliography

Adams, Ernest, "NASA Astronaut Mae Carol Jemison," flickr.com

Ahmed, Roda, *Mae Among the Stars*. New York: HarperCollins Children's Books, 2018.

Anderson, Clayton C., *The Ordinary Spaceman, from Boyhood Dreams to Astronaut,* University of Nebraska, 2015.

Calkhoven, Laurie, *(You Should Meet) Mae Jemison*. New York: Simon & Schuster, Children's Publishing Division, 2016.

Coates, James, "Riots Following the Killing of Martin Luther King, Jr.", *Chicago Tribune*, Dec. 19, 2007.

Colins, Luke, *Mae Jemison (Great African Americans),* North Mankato, MN: Pebble Books/Capstone Press, 2014.

Chow, Denise, "NASA's Shuttle Launch Steps: T-Minus 9 Minutes to Blastoff," *Human Spaceflight,* July 6, 2011.

DeSandies, Lester Kisha, "Shooting for the Stars with Dr. Mae Jemison," *Education,* April 15, 2017.

Dishman, Lydia, "The First Black Female Astronaut On Fear, Audacity, and The Importance of Inclusion," *Compass,* June 2, 2015.

Dunbar, Brian, NASA official, "Spacesuits and Spacewalks," July 5, 2018.

Hadfield, Chris, *An Astronaut's Guide to Life on Earth,* Toronto, Random House, 2013.

Jemison, Dr. Mae, "Executive Life: The Boss; What Was Space Like?" *New York Times,* Feb. 2, 2003.

Jemison, Dr. Mae, *Find Where the Wind Goes: Moments from My Life.* New York: Scholastic Press, 2001.

Jemison, Dr. Mae, "Teach Arts and Sciences Together," Ted Talks, Jan. 10, 2012.

Kelly, Scott, *Endurance, a Year in Space, a Lifetime of Discovery*, New York, Alfred A. Knopf, 2017.

Lassieur, Allison, *Astronaut Mae Jemison*. Minneapolis: Lerner Publications, 2017.

"Mae Jemison," *Chemical & Engineering News,* Vol. 85, March 26, 2007.

Massimino, Michael, *Spaceman: An Astronaut's Journey to Unlock the Secrets of the Universe.* New York: Crown Archetype, 2016.

Montgomery, Robert, "Former Astronaut Dr. Mae Jemison Empowers Youth to Explore, Connect with the World Through STEM Education," *Daily Point of Light*, June 20, 2017.

Mueller, Michael, E. and LaBalle, Candace, *Mae Jemison, Contemporary Black Biography,* encyclopedia. com, 2005.

NASA, "Apollo 10 Onboard Voice Transcription," Houston, June 1969.

NASA, "The Real Survivors," NASAexplores, May 20, 2004.

Petrahai, Zita, "An Interview with Mae Jemison," *The Dickinsonian*, April 12, 2018.

Ploscariu, Iemima, *Mae Carol Jemison, Astronaut & Educator* (Women in Science), Abdo Publishing: North Mankato, MN, 2018.

"Report of the Chicago Riot Study Committee to the Hon. Richard J. Daley," Chicago, IL, 1968. Sainato, Michael and Skojec, Chelsea, "Mae Jemison, First Black Woman in Space, Celebrates 25th Anniversary of Her Flight," *Observer*, 9/11/17.

Science Kids, "Fun Facts About the International Space Station," www.education.com

Shepherd, Jodie, *Mae Jemison* (Rookie Biographies). New York: Children's Press/Scholastic Inc., 2015.

Verger, Rob, "Here's How People Jumped Out of Planes Decades Ago—and Eject from Them Today," *Popular Science*, December 28, 2018.

AUTHOR'S NOTE

All events, facts, and characters described in this book are absolutely true, excluding the presence of, and actual quotes from, certain Feline Americans.

ABOUT THE AUTHOR

Dan Greenburg is the author of 73 books, translated into 20 languages in 24 countries, including four series of children's books: The Zack Files, Secrets of Dripping Fang, Weird Planet, and Maximum Boy. Dan's writing style uses short sentences, dialogue, humor, and cliffhangers to entice reluctant readers. Born and raised in Chicago, Dan Greenburg received a bachelor of arts degree from the University of Illinois, and his M.A. from UCLA. He lives in New York with many cats.

The Feline Historical Society Presents:
The Only True Biography of
Ben Franklin
By His Cat, Missy Hooper
With Hardly Any Help From
Dan Greenburg

A WELL-CRAFTED, FELINE-CENTRIC FRANKLIN TALE FOR YOUNG READERS.

- *KIRKUS*

If you enjoyed The Only True Biography of Mae Jemison, try the biography of Benjamin Franklin by his cat, Missy Hooper.

You probably already knew that Ben Franklin was a Founding Father of our country and a great inventor, but Missy Hooper will tell you surprising and absolutely true things that you didn't know, like:

• Why Ben had to sail to France for a dangerous secret mission to help the Colonists win the Revolutionary War.
• How Ben discovered his secretary was a British spy, and what he did about it.
• Why, if not for Ben, America would still be a British colony.

Praise for Ben Franklin Biography

"Young readers who come for the cat material will learn a lot about this famous figure" – Kirkus

"This is a perfect book for kids interested in history but also very accessible for kids who aren't. This would be a great title for reading out loud in classrooms or in the library as it will hold the attention of all the kids. An excellent title for 3rd-5th graders." – Librarian Mari Cheney